The Golden Ring

"What's so special about the ring?" I asked her.

"The lessons it taught to those who touched it and to those who were touched by it."

The Golden Ring

A Touching Christmas Story
About Giving, Faith, Love, and Loss

Written by:
JOHN SNYDER

Jacket illustration by:
Randall Quick

MOUNTAIN BREEZE PUBLISHING

OUACHITA TECHNICAL COLLEGE

Published by:

Mountain Breeze Publishing
P.O. Box 4641
Crofton, MD 21114 - 4641
A Division of
The Snyder Group, Inc.

ISBN 0-9675128-0-8

Library of Congress Card Number: 99-067125

First Mountain Breeze Publishing Trade Hardcover Printing: September 1999
10 9 8 7 6 5 4 3 2 1

Printed in the United States of America

*In memory of my father,
Joseph H. Snyder, whose company and conversation
I miss each day.*

*For my grandmother, Anna Lucile, who gave me
the inspiration to write this book.*

*And for my beautiful wife, Ruth Ellen,
my wonderful daughters, Nikki and Carli, and
the other woman in my life -
Betty Snyder, my mom.*

Prologue

Christmas. It is truly the most inspiring of holidays. It evokes in all of us an abundance of sentiments and emotions. For a brief period in our ordinarily frenzied lives, it provides us a reason to give pause and to reflect upon life, to consider where we have been, and where we are going.

Christmas instills in us a sense of peace, even in times of war. It provides us with hope in times when many are hopeless. It renews our weary spirits and rejuvenates our feelings of spirituality. It brings us closer to our God, our families, our friends ... and yes, for the most fleeting of moments, even our enemies.

It conjures up images of days gone by, of happier times in our lives that we long to recapture. It awakens our perceptions and sharpens our senses. It instills in each of us the feelings of love, giving and goodness only Christmas can bring.

The Christmas season has always been an especially extraordinary time for me. Many of my most precious remembrances are entwined in the tinsel, the glitter and the reverence of this holy season. I am blessed with a wealth of magnificent Christmas memories that will be with me always. It occurred to me that there are millions of wonderful Christmas memories locked up inside people's hearts, just waiting to be shared with anyone who will listen.

Last Christmas, I sat down with my grandmother, Anna Snyder, to share some time with her. We sat at her kitchen table and talked, as we often do, about her early years as a child and what it was like to grow up during those times. As we sipped our coffee, she told me a very moving tale about one of her childhood Christmases. It was an amazingly touching story that inspired me to write this book. Grandma is eighty-nine years old. She has kept this story to herself for all these years. What a pity it would have been if she had taken it to her grave without sharing it.

A treasure trove of wonderful Christmas stories are among us, stories that could change our lives and enrich our souls. To uncover them, we merely need to ask. Ask a grandparent or parent, an aunt or uncle to share with you their most precious Christmas memories. I encourage you to do this before the years take your loved ones from you, and these remembrances will be lost, tragically, forever.

❋ ❋ ❋

Chapter I

A heavy mist chilled the morning air. The Christmas snow, which had fallen just a few days before, was beginning to melt. A curtain of gray fog rose steadily from the thawing blanket of white, lifting into the cold and lifeless sky. The bald oak trees that lined the backyard stood dripping with thaw, their ashen bark blending into the drab countryside. The scene had the mystic quality of a faded dream.

The cold damp air leaked through the back door and crept up my spine, bringing a shiver that woke me from my daydream. Reaching for a leftover Christmas cookie on the plate before me, I watched her as she cautiously shuffled across the kitchen floor. The dismal light of the morning trickled into the room through the window where she stood, casting her image into a silhouette. Her delicate frame was hunched over at the shoulders as she poured hot coffee into a cup. Her hand trembled slightly as she carefully placed the mug on the table.

"Here, Johnny," she said in a hoarse voice. "This ought to warm you up."

Her caring smile was enough to chase the chill away and make the dreary day seem filled with sunshine. She returned to the coffeepot and drew another cup for herself. As she took her place at the table, it became more apparent that the years were catching up to her. She raised the cup to her weathered lips and took her first sip of coffee. It was then that I noticed something on the little finger of her right hand that I had never seen before - a stunning gold ring with an unusual ruby setting.

"That's a pretty ring, Grandma. I don't think I've ever seen you wear it before. Was it a Christmas gift this year?"

She paused and looked down at the ring, twisting it slightly with the fingers of her other hand. She sat in silence for a moment, then looked up and said, "Yes it was a Christmas gift, but not from this year. I received it many Christmases ago, eighty to be exact, when I was about nine years old."

"And you've had it all this time?"

"Yes, but I haven't worn it in years because it didn't fit for a long time. But I guess these tired old fingers of mine are shrinking a bit. I tried it on Christmas morning and it fit on my pinkie just fine," she said, holding the ring out to admire it. "This is a very special ring, John."

"Who gave it to you?"

"My father, bless his soul. Every Christmas, I take this ring out of my jewelry box and hold it for a while. It helps me remember that special Christmas Day so many years ago when my father gave it to me."

"What's so special about the ring?" I asked her.

"The lessons it taught to those who touched it and to those who were touched by it."

"What do you mean?"

"This ring has a mysterious past. The events that led up to my father giving it to me, and the place where he got it are mysterious as well."

"Mysterious? Where did he get it?"

"Wait," she said, as she put her hands on mine. "I'll tell you the incredible story behind this remarkable ring."

Grandma clutched my hands and looked into my eyes. Her wrinkled face and silver hair reflected the many years that had passed since she received the gift of the golden ring. She began to tell me the story, and I had a strong sense of being pulled back in time. As I looked deeper into her eyes, the wrinkles seemed to fade and the face of a little girl with curly brown hair and brilliant blue eyes began to emerge.

Chapter II

It was a cold December evening in 1918, only four days before Christmas. The winter sun had set about an hour before over the small borough of Myersdale, a picturesque township nestled in the dense snow-covered mountains of western Pennsylvania's coal country. The spirit of Christmas was in the air, particularly at 525 North Street, where the Beal family resided.

The six Beal children had done all they could to hurry the winter days along to reach the threshold of Christmas. Once there, they strived to keep themselves in the moment, pressing their parents' patience nightly with ingenious schemes to stay up a little longer, to revel a bit more in the present.

"I forgot to feed Nelly," one would call out from an upstairs bedroom, referring to the family's beagle. In truth, the plumpish pooch could have skipped a week of vittles and would have been no worse off.

Anna, the middle child, was nine years old. Her long brown curly hair hung in obstinate ringlets around her face. Her blue eyes sparkled with the anticipation of Christmas, a very special holiday in her heart. She loved the sweet smells created by her mother's holiday baking, the tangy scent of a fresh-cut Christmas tree and the

17

soothing sounds of Christmas carols sung in church and on street corners. Anna delighted in looking at Christmas decorations. By the holiday's end, her nose print was on most of the shop windows in Myersdale, as she pressed her schnozzle against the glass for a closer look at the decorations inside.

When she thought about what Santa would bring, her stomach got that feeling she felt when her father pushed her high on the swing in the backyard under the large maple tree. Most of all, she treasured the warm and peaceful feeling which swept over her and all those around her at this time of year. She enjoyed the way people treated each other so nicely as Christmas approached, and missed this fellowship that sadly seemed to fade after the Yuletide.

Anna was quiet by nature; one could never discern what complex thoughts were behind her pensive frown. She followed a ritual on these cold evenings. She would walk to the living room window made opaque by the ice etchings artfully carved by Jack Frost. Warming the frozen crystals with the palm of her hand, she would stare out into the approaching darkness.

Fresh snow covered the streets of the town. The recent snowfall clung to the tree limbs causing them to bow under the weight. The white powder glistened under the gentle glow of the streetlights, appearing as diamond dust glittering in the night. The air was frigid, but unusually still, a perfect background for the church bells that could be heard ringing in the season.

In the distance, the whistle of a train echoed faintly through the hollow. It sounded again with more measure. Its high-pitched bellow, growing ever closer, announced the arrival of an incoming train. The rumble of the approaching engine became louder as it shook the tracks leading into town.

The heat from the coal-fired potbelly stove warmed Anna's back as she faced the frosty window. The sound of laughter ricocheted through the large house on North Street, interrupted by the periodic squealing of Anna's older sisters as they ran around the house, chased by the younger brother they affectionately called "Boopie". Elwood was his real name. His older brother, Earl, took the name Boopie from a character he saw in a movie. He tagged his little brother with it, and, unfortunately for Elwood, the nickname caught on around town and stuck with him the rest of his life.

Boopie had always been the mischievous one of the family. He was also the only blonde, and his pale locks were often seen bouncing through the house like a streak of yellow lightning. And, just as most lightning is followed by thunder, Boopie's streak through the house was usually followed by the discovery of some playful prank.

Mabel and Jule, Anna's older sisters, were very much alike. Mabel, who went by the name "Sis", was a good three years older than Jule, but the girls' features were nearly identical. Each had a tiny freckle on the left cheek that Anna used to try to mimic, with little success, using a pencil lead. Both sisters were also very boister-

19

ous, a vast difference from Anna's disposition. Despite the obvious differences between Anna and her sisters, the three of them remained close.

"No running in the house!" shouted Anna's mother, Elda, as she looked up briefly from peeling a potato. She tried to project her voice with authority, but she was unable to hide her smile; she shared her children's excitement about the approaching holiday.

Anna, as usual, was oblivious to the commotion within the house as she continued to gaze pensively out the window. Boopie, Anna's junior by a year, sneaked up behind his big sister and startled her by tickling her under her arms.

"Oh!" Anna shouted with surprise. By the time she could turn around to retaliate, the culprit was already running up the stairs in search of someone else to pester.

This would be anybody but Earl, the oldest brother, partly because he was rarely at home anymore, and partly because he had discovered the art of indifference. Much to Boopie's dismay, Earl's attitude tended to squelch his pranks.

"Thanks, Boop." Earl would holler when he found frogs in one of his drawers. He would then quietly release the creatures back into the night. Or, "What a kidder," Earl would intone when he returned from work and his little brother would jump out from behind the couch in an attempt to startle him.

This time the object of Boopie's newest attack was obviously Jule, as her alto *"Boooooopppiieee!"* resounded throughout the top floor.

Once more, Anna directed her attention outside. Her warm breath steamed the window and it quickly began to freeze. As she wiped away the icy crystals, she watched the blurred figure of a man walking down North Street from the train station where he had just arrived. It was her father, Joseph.

His large frame cast a massive shadow in the moonlit darkness as he trudged through the new fallen snow. His image, at first, appeared almost gargoyle-like as it lumbered to and fro, moving from light to shadow. The pace of Anna's heart quickened as her father drew nearer. She watched him emerge from the shadows and recalled many holiday memories: the Christmas he made the wooden manger scene, the year he took all the children sledding, and last Christmas, when he gave the Christmas prayer at church, telling the Christmas story to the entire congregation.

To Anna, Joseph was a hero. He could fix anything. When Tobi, her mischievous cat, disappeared one rainy night, her father braved the squall and returned hours later, drenched, but with Tobi safely tucked under his arm, warm and dry, carefully wrapped in his coat.

When her father neared the house, Anna saw the steam coming from his nose and mouth as he breathed. Joseph had just put in his customary twelve-hour day on the B&O Railroad, where he worked as an engineer. Anna could tell by his plodding gait that this had been an especially tiring day. Seeing the warm glow of light in the windows of his house gave Joseph cause to hasten his tired pace.

With each step, Anna's excitement grew. She could hear her father's footsteps as they crunched into the crisp white powder. Anna couldn't contain herself any longer. "Daddy!" she screamed. "He's home!"

The announcement caused a stampede toward the front door. Anna, Sis, Jule, Boopie, and even young Dick jostled for position in the vestibule. Joseph's steel-toed work boots sounded like large kettledrums as they hit each wooden step on the front porch. He stopped to stomp the snow off his feet, causing the glass in the front door to vibrate and letting Elda know he was home.

Joseph peered through the etched glass window on the front door and caught his first glimpse of the welcoming party. Despite his current state of exhaustion, he managed a warm smile as he anticipated the playful mauling by his children. He swung the door open and the children shouted in unison, "Merry Christmas, Daddy!"

"Hey, kids!" Joseph shouted with a broad smile. "Have I got a surprise for you."

This prompted a confused chatter as the children tried to unravel the mystery. "What is it? What is it?" Jule shouted repeatedly, louder and louder. When Boopie attempted to out-yell his sister, his voice suddenly cracked with a duck-like sound, causing him to become the target of everyone's laughter.

"Hey, Boopie, ever think about trying out for the church choir?" taunted Sis.

With that, Joseph pulled a wrinkled paper sack from his right coat pocket and teased, "Okay, it's something to eat, it's sweet, it's red and green and..."

... "And your mother will be upset if you eat it before supper!" Elda said with a grin, as she rounded the corner from the kitchen. Boopie quickly grabbed the bag and streaked into the living room, pursued closely by the other children.

Joseph took off his coat, which was heavy with moisture, and hung it on the oak coat tree in the hall. The heat from the stove was a comfort to his frostbitten face. The welcome smell of supper cooking defrosted his nostrils as he walked into the kitchen where Elda was hurrying the evening meal. He walked toward her, wrapping his arms around her from behind while she whisked the gravy on the stove.

"Joseph," she scolded playfully. "How long have we been married now?"

"Not long enough?" he queried, trying to make his wife smile.

"Seventeen years," she answered for him, not looking at his face to avoid losing her resolve. "And for how many of those years have we had children?"

"Let's see," Joseph said, making a murmuring count of Earl's age. "Too many?" he joked, making his wife swing around in mock surprise. "I mean, sixteen."

She stepped toward him, wiping her hands on her

apron. "And of those sixteen, how many times have I let you give the children c-a-n-d-y before supper?" her eyebrow was raised.

"Speaking of supper, honey, it sure smells delicious," he said shaking his head. "You must have been cooking all day!"

"Oh, you," she said, ruffling his hair. "Always changing the subject."

Sneakily, Joseph reached around behind her and swiped some chocolate icing from the freshly baked cake that was sitting on the counter.

"Hey, you're not exempt from the no-sweets-before-supper rule!" Elda said sternly, but she laughed as Joseph sucked the icing from his finger.

"Good cake though," he said grinning, as Elda made the announcement to the rest of the family that supper was ready.

"Hey, where's Earl?" asked Joseph.

Earl worked at a nearby furniture factory running a lathe and keeping the floor clear of wood shavings and sawdust. He was usually home by now.

"He should be here any minute," answered Elda, knowing that it was a rare occasion for Earl to miss a home-cooked meal. Just as she finished making that prediction, the back door burst open.

"Your ears burning, son?" asked Joseph, smiling.

"No sir, but my stomach is growlin' like a train!" answered Earl shucking off his coat and gloves. Earl was a jovial sort. His round crimson face appeared even more so this night after his long walk in the cold night air. He loudly greeted everyone at the table as he bounced his fist lightly on his siblings' heads. Before sitting down, he gave a slight tug to the right ear of his younger brother, Dick, who seemed to be staring off into space.

"What's up, daydreamer? You thinking about Santa or Evelyn Ritchie's pigtails?" Earl teased.

Dick, at age five, was the youngest of the Beal clan. The most silent of the bunch, he related most to Anna, except he was even more shy. He idolized his oldest brother's gregarious nature, and even at this early age, tried, unsuccessfully, to mimic Earl's traits. His attempts at off-the-cuff humor landed flat more often then not, but he still got sympathetic smiles for trying. When this happened, he would retreat back into himself for a while, only to try again later. Eventually, he got it right, and he would grow up to be most like his older brother.

Earl zealously plunged his fork into the mountain of mashed potatoes on his plate and piloted it toward his mouth. One stern look from his father reminded him that he was doing something out of turn. Joseph cleared his throat prompting Earl to stop and knock the potatoes off his fork. Sheepishly, he returned the utensil to its original position beside his plate.

As the Beals solemnly bowed their heads, Joseph offered the blessing and his annual reminder that the true reason for their happiness at the holidays was not Santa or presents, but rather family and, most importantly, the birth of Jesus.

The prayer, as intended, cast a serious note on the table. It wasn't that Joseph wanted to bring everyone's spirits down; he just felt that somewhere amid the sparkling lights and exuberant giggles, the true meaning of Christmas was being lost.

Chapter III

After dinner, the girls helped their mother clear the table and wash the dishes. Earl tended the fire while Boopie interrogated his father in the living room about the events of his lengthy day on the railroad.

"Hey, Dad, what happens when it snows a lot on the train tracks; can the train still go?"

"Well, it depends. If the snow isn't too deep or heavy with water, then it usually can."

"What happens if there's a lot of snow, piled real high?" the interrogation continued.

"In that case, if the snow is too heavy to run the train through, they call out the snow fighters."

"Snow fighters?" Boopie cocked his head.

"Yes, it's a crew that drives a special train engine which has a big plow on the front. It plows through snow drifts to clear the tracks."

"Oh," said Boopie wiping his nose with an upward swipe of his palm, "I think I want to be a snow fighter someday so I can drive a train through a big pile of snow - as big as a mountain - and make it explode into a big white cloud!" With this, he raised his arms in a circle and made a noise like a loud explosion, accidentally knocking the candy dish off the table with the emphatic motion of his arms.

His father laughed. "Well, Boop, I don't think life on the railroad is always that exciting; usually it's little more than back-breaking work. Why don't you study hard and be a doctor? That way you can spend lots of time with your family and make a lot more money."

Overhearing the conversation, Earl said, "Sure, and deal with a bunch of sick people coughing on you and blood everywhere. No thanks. Give me the railroad."

"Don't knock the medical profession too much. If it wasn't for Dr. Towles, Boopie wouldn't even be here," Joseph said.

"Huh? What do you mean, Dad?" asked Boopie, squinting at his father.

"Well, you were wriggling around from the moment you entered this world and even before! You wriggled so much you darn near hung yourself on your cord. Took the doc almost an hour to get you untangled. Without him, you may have choked!" Joseph told him.

"Cord?" Boopie asked. "What cord?"

"Never mind," Joseph said, attempting to close the door on the conversation that he just opened.

Boopie looked quizzically at him and then at Earl. "You remember that?"

"How could I?" said Earl, "I was just Dick's age when all that happened. But I wouldn't put it past you."

Boopie turned his glance to his father, who was nodding slowly. "It's true," said Joseph. "Go ask your mother if you don't believe me," figuring he'd let Elda explain about the cord in the event the subject resurfaced.

"No, I believe you. I just didn't think about doctors like that.

Maybe I'll be a doctor when I grow up and I'll be the town hero!" he shouted. Curling his arms up over his shoulders, he pumped his muscles, then shot from the room, seeking out his sisters to tell them his near-death story.

The fire popped like corn as Earl added another log. Behind him, young Dick mimicked every move, prodding the air with an imaginary poker, blowing on the embers until his cheeks glowed a bright pink. He even grunted as he pretended to load more wood onto the imaginary blaze.

Earl waited until he heard Boopie in the kitchen shouting his story. "Did you make all that up?"

"No," laughed Joseph. "What a reputation I must have in this family!"

"Tell me a story about me then. What was I like when I was little?"

"Look behind you," said Joseph motioning toward Earl's youngest brother. "That was you following me. You did everything I did, watching the way I washed my face, even wanting to go to the outhouse when I did." Earl blushed as he laughed, then forced a cough in an attempt to disguise his embarrassment.

"Why do you think I kept having kids? I needed another boy to get you off my back!" Joseph kidded.

With that, father and son shared a laugh. Then young Dick climbed up on Earl's back, wrapping his arms around his big brother's neck.

"Looks like it worked," joked Earl. Then in a more serious tone, he asked, "So, how was the railroad today?"

Before long, Joseph was spinning railroad yarns, his sons

gathered around him, listening. After hearing a few railroad stories, Earl began to recount his day at the furniture factory. The audience was far less intrigued, except for young Dick, who listened intently from under the bridge of Earl's right leg, which was propped up on the table in front of the sofa.

"How many chairs did you make today?" asked Dick.

"I didn't make any. But I turned legs for a whole bunch of tables."

Joseph's attention slowly drifted away from Earl's account of his workday. It had been a long week, and he couldn't help thinking how he would spend his time over the next few days. He had the weekend off, a rare occasion indeed. It was unusual for him to be off two days in a row, much less over a weekend. He was happy that he could spend the next two days, so close to the holidays, with his family.

"The Johnsons said I could borrow their truck tomorrow if we wanted to go pick out a Christmas tree," Earl said.

The Johnsons lived two doors down and were one of the few families on North Street who owned a motorized vehicle. They were the ones who had everything first, but they were very generous, lending their possessions to their neighbors whenever possible. On several occasions Joseph had borrowed tools from Tom Johnson that had cut his workload in half. With Joseph's limited amount of free time, having the Johnsons as neighbors was a blessing.

"Again?" harrumphed Joseph, his mood shifting away from the happy complacency of earlier. "I thought they lent you that truck just last weekend?"

"They did." Earl said flatly. "But how else would we manage

to get that tree home?"

"I don't know why you have to go to so much trouble to hack down a tree and lug it back here, getting all those needles all over the place."

"Well, I was hunting the other day on the Saunders farm and Mr. Saunders said I could pick out any tree I wanted," offered Earl. "So it would be silly not to get one, Dad. Besides, I like a tree, and so do Mom and the kids. You should come with us this time; I bet you'd be able to pick the best tree yet."

"You know how I feel about all of this silly Christmas stuff," Joseph answered. "I'll help you set up the manger, but that's it. I won't decorate any tree!"

Earl certainly did know how his father felt about Christmas. He just didn't understand how his father could love the holiday as much as he did and yet refuse to participate in any part of it other than the religious aspect. Joseph wasn't an obstinate man, but he always held true to his beliefs. And Joseph did not believe that Christmas should be anything other than a celebration of the birth of Christ, plain and simple. His strict religious upbringing had stuck with him. As a child, he knew nothing of Santa Claus, holiday gifts, or Christmas trees. Oddly, it was his steadfastness in his beliefs that earned the respect of his children, but they were still children and disappointed that their father didn't share in every dimension of their joy.

Joseph's Christmas was truly one-dimensional. He had never given gifts at Christmas, even to his children. He did, however, tolerate their belief in this fellow Kris Kringle. He never really told them there was no Santa Claus, he just never acknowledged that there was. He tried to understand his children's fas-

31

cination with the jolly old elf and did what he could, within his own bounds, to help Elda ready the house for the holiday.

Oh, Santa did visit the Beal household. Every Christmas Eve, after the children had gone to bed, Elda would lug in a huge fir tree and decorate it gloriously to commemorate the occasion. And she always made certain that an abundance of presents were under the tree to be opened on Christmas morning.

❄ ❄ ❄

In the kitchen, the girls were finishing up their chores. Their mother disappeared for a few minutes and then emerged from the cellar with a box of chestnuts for roasting. After toasting the nuts slowly on the stove, Anna, Sis, and Jule followed their mother into the living room and proudly presented the bounty to their father and brothers. The family sat around the small sofa table talking and joking with each other. Anna took her usual position on her father's left. This is how the Beal family spent many winter evenings, this one no exception.

The talk soon turned to Christmas, as the children tried to imagine what Santa would be delivering in his sleigh.

"Will you read us the Christmas story, Daddy?" asked Anna.

Joseph, although tremendously tired, reached for the Bible that he kept on the table next to his chair. Thumbing through the pages of the New Testament, he began reading the accounts of the birth of Jesus from the books of Matthew and Luke. Joseph's sometimes-stern voice always softened when he read from the Bible. This was fortuitous for two reasons: first, it helped bring the words closer to his children and second, the tone of his voice almost always lulled them into a sleepy trance.

After the story was finished and the chestnuts were gone, Elda playfully chased the children upstairs to bed. Joseph accompanied them, tucking in each one of them and making sure they all said their prayers. He headed back down the stairs and heard a voice trailing behind him.

"G'nite, Daddy, I love you." It was Anna, the most affectionate child Joseph had ever known. She also had a sense of kindness that was well beyond her years. While all of his children excelled at something, Joseph took great pride in the fact that his daughter was one of the most selfless people he knew, adults included.

There was a chorus of giggling as the rest of the gaggle - Dick, Boopie, Sis, and Jule - each said their individual good nights, an obvious, but unsuccessful stall tactic, meant to delay the sandman.

"Good night, my crafty children. Now get some sleep," Joseph teased. As he walked down the last few steps of the intricate wooden staircase that adorned the foyer, he couldn't help grinning when he thought about his children's holiday enthusiasm.

When Joseph returned to the living room, he saw his wife curled up on the sofa, smiling as she deftly worked the knitting needle through the ball of yarn on her lap. Joseph picked up his Bible and began reading where he'd left off.

"Got a twitchy face tonight?" Joseph inquired, referring to Elda's repeated smiles.

"Oh, I was just thinking."

"Hm, I know what that means."

"Whatever do you mean?" asked Elda, coyly.

Joseph responded with a knowing smile.

"Well," Elda continued, knowing she was found out, "I heard Earl ask you about helping us cut the Christmas tree tomorrow."

"And let me guess. You want me to go along?"

"Come on, it will be fun."

"I can't, Elda you know how I feel. It would be against everything I've stood for."

"I know. I just thought maybe you'd make an exception this year, just to pick the tree. You don't have to decorate it or..."

Joseph cut her off in midsentence. "I don't really think its such a good idea. This year it'll be the tree, next year it'll be presents, and then the whole holiday will mean something different for me, and I'm not prepared to compromise it like that."

"Just tell me you'll think about it."

"I'll think about it."

Elda leaned over and kissed him good night. "Thanks," she said, smiling down at him. "Are you coming up to bed?"

"No. I think I'll stay up and read for a while longer. I'll be up soon."

The time passed quickly and Joseph's eyes became heavy with sleep. His head began to nod forward and then back. When he caught himself drifting off, he would jerk sharply in an effort to stay awake. After trying to fight off sleep for several minutes, Joseph noticed a brilliant white light glowing from the direction of the kitchen. He heard the faint sound of a sweet but unfamiliar melody. The bright luminescence moved slowly toward him, the music sounding ever louder. He rubbed his eyes in an effort to clear his vision and tried to focus on the hazy figure of a man with a long brown beard that fell in an assemblage of curls at his chest. The figure stood before Joseph in silence.

"My God!" Joseph gasped aloud. He could not believe what he was witnessing. The image before him was that of Jesus Christ. Joseph's jaw dropped in bewilderment. Then the spirit held out something in its hand and spoke for the first time. Joseph could barely make out the apparition's cryptic message.

"Joseph, take this gift from me to you as a token of my love. It was a gift of gold given to me by one of the wise men at the manger the night I was born in Bethlehem. It does me no good, yet it will bring others great joy."

Joseph nervously extended his right hand to meet the outstretched hand of the figure. The Spirit was offering him a beautiful golden ring. Joseph's hand was trembling. Then an angel appeared and said, "Fear not, for behold, we bring you good tidings of great joy."

As Joseph reached out for the ring, a loud thud caused him to sit up abruptly. Just as suddenly as they had appeared, the heavenly images vanished and the music stopped. Joseph had dozed off momentarily. His Bible had slipped from his grasp and fallen to the floor, awakening him.

The hallucination left Joseph shaken. It had seemed so real. In fact, in the initial moments after the event, he questioned whether it was a dream or reality.

"Naaaa," he grumbled, trying to reassure himself. "I must be more tired than I thought." He retrieved the Bible from the floor and placed it on the table. He convinced himself that it was a dream, probably induced by the hard day's work and the comforting warmth of the fire radiating from the potbelly stove.

Joseph collected himself and walked upstairs to his bedroom for what would be a restless night of tossing and turning. He could not stop thinking about the dream. Each time he fell asleep, he would hear the beautiful music and the vision would return. He always woke up at the same point in the dream, reaching for the golden ring in Jesus' outstretched hand. Finally, Joseph fell into a welcome state of uninterrupted slumber.

Chapter IV

The smell of frying eggs and bacon, pancakes, and freshly brewed coffee wafted up the stairs into Joseph's bedroom where it awakened his senses. The night had not been kind to him. Elda had let him sleep late.

It was after nine when Joseph stumbled down the stairs, embarrassed by his late awakening. Joseph was usually up at five A.M. Even on his days off, he rarely slept in. Elda wondered what could have caused the sudden shift in her husband's behavior. She was putting the finishing touches on the family's breakfast when Joseph entered the kitchen, yawning.

"You must have really been thinking hard on what we talked about last night. You were tossing like a hung sheet in a wind storm," Elda said, half-jokingly.

Joseph mustered up a muted smile to respond. "Well, you know, I'm a thoughtful guy."

Elda wanted Joseph to talk about what was on his mind, but she didn't want to pry, so instead let it drop.

"Why don't you call our rascals in for breakfast?" Elda asked.

Joseph stuck his head out the kitchen door, which led to the backyard. The children were in the midst of building a misshaped snowman when Joseph called them to eat.

"Can't we stay out a little longer? We're almost done," pleaded Anna from across the yard. Her request was fortified by a chorus of pleas from the rest of the construction crew.

"You're not snowmen, you know. You need to eat some hot food, and your mother has seen to it that you get some this mor…"

"Hey, Dad!" Earl yelled from behind the hedge.

When Joseph turned to look, he was pelted in the forehead by a huge snowball sent special delivery to him from Earl.

"Bulls-eye!" shouted Earl with pride, as the missle connected with its target. The children laughed hysterically.

Joseph immediately bolted from the back porch toward Earl, snow still clumped over his brow. Laughing, he ran toward his son, gathered snow from the tops of the hedges that lined the yard. Earl had a sizable head start. He retreated, elbows thrashing high as he ran through the snow, knowing how swiftly his father could run and how deadly his aim.

Joseph's first attempt uncharacteristically missed its mark and whizzed past Earl's head. He fired another as he ran. Suddenly, Earl felt the tip of his ear sting with cold. It was merely a flesh wound, he thought, continuing his getaway. Then he took a direct hit to the buttocks and another to the back. He turned to see if his father was gaining on him and received a mouthful when a snowball landed and broke on his left cheek.

"Okay! Okay! I give up!" Earl surrendered.

"See? That'll teach you to mess with your old man!" wheezed Joseph, coming up behind his son. Earl spit out the remains of the snowball and looked at his father, who was hunched over in a panting fatigue, his hands resting on his knees. Joseph returned the glance and they both began to laugh. Joseph stood upright and put his arm around his son; the two walked toward the house where Elda was waiting.

"Seriously, Joseph, you'd think you were a child yourself, chasing after poor Earl like that. Come here, Honey," she cooed to her son. Earl played along, grabbing her around the waist and sticking out his bottom lip in a forced pout.

"Did Daddy hurt you?" Elda teased her nearly grown son. Joseph ran up to her other side to join in.

"He hit me first, Mom!" mocked Joseph.

"The two of you! Am I going to have to ask Anna to watch the two of you when I'm not around?"

Upon hearing this, a smile blossomed on Anna's face. The thought of being in charge of her elders was overpowering.

"Oh yes!" cried Sis, "And she doesn't miss on the first try!" referring to her father's initial snowball toss that missed its mark.

Joseph lunged toward his daughter and tickled her until she retracted her statement.

"I was only kidding, Daddy. Honest, you're the best shot in the whole wide world!"

"Let's go in, or our breakfast will get cold," Elda said, herding the family toward the back door.

Filing into the kitchen, they all got a whiff of the warm meal that awaited them. Joseph asked Earl to say the morning blessing. Earl obliged and then, with a mouthful of biscuit, announced, "What a great day to pick out a tree!"

"What kind of tree are we going to get this year?" asked Boopie.

"A Christmas tree, silly," young Dick replied sincerely, causing the entire table to erupt with laughter.

"Yeah, but I want one that has needles that smell up the whole house!" exclaimed Anna.

"And one that's the color of Mom's favorite sweater," noted Jule.

"One sooooo biiiigggg the top hits the ceiling!" said Boopie, gesturing with his hands and almost upending his milk glass.

Elda sipped her tea and watched the expression on Joseph's face.

"Anybody want to help me split firewood?" Joseph asked, trying, unsuccessfully, to change the subject. Luckily for him, the remainder of the meal was dedicated to planning the final details of the trip. It looked, for the moment, as though he had escaped being put on the spot. Then Earl piped up, "Dad, you going with us today?"

"Oh yes, please, Daddy?" said young Dick. Then the rest of the children joined in, all pleading with him to go.

"No. I've got tons of chores to do this morning."

The children kept nudging him, but he wouldn't give. "I'll tell you what, kids," he said. "Why don't you go out and finish your snowman, and I'll help your mother clean up the dishes." Before he could finish his sentence, the table was vacated and the kitchen door slammed shut as the children dashed back outside to complete their artful creation.

The kitchen was silent while Joseph cleared the table and handed Elda the dishes for washing.

"Joseph..."

"I know what you're going to say, Elda, and I can't go."

"You can't, or you won't?" Elda countered.

"I can't *and* I won't," Joseph said bluntly.

There was a strained silence between Joseph and Elda as they cleaned up the last of the dishes. Joseph went upstairs to shave and wash up. Elda finished tidying up the kitchen.

❄ ❄ ❄

Joseph lifted the razor to his face and paused at his reflection in the mirror. He thought about the dream he had the night before; its meaning eluded him. Why was Jesus trying to give him a ring? Guiding the razor carefully over his face, he considered his family's request that he go with them to pick out a Christmas tree. "Should I go?" He asked himself silently. He debated the question internally, back and forth, for the remainder of his shave. "It would be fun, but I'd be going against my beliefs" ..."What could it harm?" ... "I'd probably have to start decorating it next year. No. No, I just shouldn't," he thought.

Joseph finished shaving, got dressed, and went back downstairs. The children and Elda were assembled in the vestibule, buttoning up in preparation for their day in the cold. Earl was heading out the door to borrow the Johnson's truck.

"You sure you won't change your mind and come with us, Dad?" Earl asked once more.

"Yeah, I'm sure. You all go on without me."

Joseph walked out to the kitchen where he sat on a chair and pulled on his boots. He heard Earl drive up in front of the house. As the truck stopped, the brakes screeched and the exhaust backfired. The front door whined as it closed, cutting off the sounds of his children's laughter and excitement. He sat there for an instant, looking out the window at the snowman in the backyard. Then he arose hastily, grabbed his coat and hat, and took off in pursuit of his family. As he opened the front door, Earl drove off, unaware of his father's change of heart. Unfortunately, it had come too late; they were gone.

Somewhat dejected, Joseph sat down on the front porch steps. "How foolish to have waited so long to make up your mind, you stubborn fool," he scolded himself aloud. How he wished he had not been so headstrong. If he hadn't, he would be laughing with his children right now as they all rode in the truck, bound for a festive adventure in the woods. He pictured what it would have been like. He imagined Anna on his lap, young Dick tugging at his pant leg. He could almost hear Boopie's zestful shouts and the giggles of Sis and Jule.

Anna's cat jumped up into his lap, giving him a fright and breaking his concentration. "Gee, Tobi!" he gasped. "You scared me to death."

Not terribly fond of cats, Joseph did find some comfort in the animal's attention, listening to it purr as it weaved a path between his feet. He stroked Tobi's fur and his earlier troubling thoughts returned. He was confused by his feelings. His steadfast beliefs were at odds with his desire to be with the ones he loved, to share in their innocent enthusiasm. Then, he concluded aloud, "Oh well, it's probably better this way."

He stared up at the morning sky for a moment, then, petting Tobi on the head said, "Well, boy, I guess it's just you and me. Let's get to splittin' that firewood."

Just then, he heard a loud backfire and looked up to see the Johnson's black Ford truck coming down the street. Earl pulled up and honked the horn. Anna jumped from the back of the truck and ran toward the house. She streaked passed Joseph on her way to the front door and blurted out, "I forgot my mittens!"

"Hurry up, Anna!" Earl shouted impatiently from the driver's side window of the truck.

In a minute, Anna was out the front door again with her mittens. As she whizzed past Joseph, he grabbed her and swung her around.

"How about if I go along?" he said.

Anna's face immediately lit up with her approval.

"Oh, Daddy, will you?"

"I sure will!"

Anna took his hand and pulled him toward the truck. Joseph lifted her aboard, then he climbed into the back of the truck himself, where he was met with a warm reception.

Earl and Elda, who were in the truck's cab, turned and looked at Joseph through the window as he took his seat in the truck's bed. He returned their looks and gave them a conciliatory wink. Earl and his mother looked at each other and smiled.

The truck drove up North Street, turned left at the corner, and began its short journey to the Saunders farm. In the back of the truck, Joseph and the children sang Christmas carols. Elda stared out the window, her face beaming with contentment.

Chapter V

*T*he Beal's arrival at the farm was broadcast by a thunderous backfire from the Johnson's truck, which startled everyone from their seats. The blast sent the cows scattering and gave Bob Saunders cause to look out his window.

The Saunders family had been friendly with the Beals for years. Bob Saunders was a generous man who owned about five hundred acres of beautiful land on which he raised cattle. Also on the property was a large evergreen grove with some of the most exquisite fir trees in all of Pennsylvania. The grove provided Myersdale with many of its Christmas trees each year.

The truck bounced and shook as it careened over the deep ruts that were worn into the ice in front of the house. Bob met the truck as it coasted to a stop not far from the large porch that wrapped around the building. He was a burly man with an unruly reddish-brown mustache that covered his upper lip. His insubordinate stache was matched by an abundant set of eyebrows, which shaded his forehead. Thumbing his red suspenders, Bob approached the truck with amusement.

"Howdy," he said with a welcoming grin. "Is this the Christmas tree expedition?"

Joseph rose from the bed of the truck, making himself visible to Bob for the first time. "Hey there, Bob!"

Bob was surprised to see him. He was aware of Joseph's aversion to Christmas trees and the like.

"What brings you out on a cold day like today?" Bob asked. Surely, he thought, Joseph's not here to cut a Christmas tree.

"Daddy's going to help us pick the tree," Anna volunteered.

"You're kidding!" Bob said with astonishment, looking straight at Joseph.

"Well, I guess I couldn't escape this year. They had me surrounded," Joseph said with a laugh. He was feeling a bit uneasy and slightly embarrassed by all the commotion.

"You all look like you're frozen," Bob exclaimed. "Come on in the house and I'll warm you up with a cup of Julia's hot apple cider."

"That's an invitation you won't have to repeat," Elda said, her voice quivering from the cold.

"Well, let's go then," Bob replied, leading the group toward the front door.

Once inside, everyone huddled around the fireplace, which held a comforting blaze. The rough oak mantle was decorated with pine garland from the grove, meticulously arranged by Bob's wife, Julia.

Julia was a petite woman, blessed with an hourglass figure. She had extremely fair skin, stunning blue eyes, and blonde hair. Bob and Julia made a very handsome couple. She was an excellent homemaker and had a splendid talent for decorating and crafts. She loved children but, sadly, was unable to conceive any of her own. It always lifted her spirits when the Beals came to visit. She treasured the time with the children, and they delighted in the way she doted on them.

Julia entered the room carrying a tray of hot cider. The

steam from the beverage filled the air, mixing the scents of apple and pine. She made sure each of the children got one of her sugar cookies, too.

"Boy, these are good! Can I have another one?" blurted Boopie.

"Boopie!" his mother scolded.

"That's alright, Elda, he can have another, if it's okay with you, that is."

"What do you say, Boopie?"

"Please, Mrs. Saunders, may I have another cookie? Please? Please?"

"Joseph, I heard they are going to expand the railroad yard. Is that true?" Bob asked.

"That's what I hear. There's a new coal-mining operation opening up. We'll be running more trainloads of coal out of here. I suppose it's for the good."

"It'll certainly be good for Elliott's Hardware and Lumber, that's for sure"

"Yeah, I remember when my daddy could have been partners with old man Elliott, but they could never get along. Sure would be nice to have your own store and not have to work for someone else."

"Ah, Joseph, the railroad's been pretty good to you."

"Yes, but it's hard work and the hours are long."

"Can we go now?" interrupted young Dick, tugging on his father's arm.

"Yeah, Daddy, it's hot in here," complained Boopie. "Can we go outside?"

Joseph's feet had just begun to thaw. He was comfortable

there by the fire, with a cup of warm apple cider cradled in his hands. The prospect of going back out into the cold morning air was somewhat less than appealing, but he yielded to his children's enthusiasm.

Anna tugged at his hand. "Come on, Daddy. Let's go find a pretty tree."

Joseph downed the remainder of his cider and placed the cup on the table. While everyone bundled up in preparation, Bob told them, "There's a sled out by the barn you can use to carry the tree down off the mountain. I'm sure you'll be able to find a tree that suits you. There are a number of beauties up there. Take the one you want and Merry Christmas."

Bob and Julia ushered them to the front door and the expedition began. Earl led the way, pulling the sled behind him. He was familiar with the farm, because he hunted there frequently. Young Dick and Boopie hitched a ride on the sled. Anna and her sisters followed, while Joseph and Elda walked behind.

Elda slid her glove-covered palm into the grasp of Joseph's large hand. She looked up at him while they walked and said, "Thank you, Joseph. This means a lot to the children. And it means more to me than you'll ever be able to understand."

He looked down at her and smiled, then gave her tiny hand a gentle squeeze without saying a word.

It was a beautiful day. The sun reflected brightly off the white snow. The sky was a lucid blue with no clouds in sight. The December wind was still cutting, though, sweeping across the fields and blasting the loose snow into their faces.

When they approached the top of the first hill, Earl stopped suddenly, holding up his hand as a signal for everyone to freeze.

"Sh!" Earl said as he turned around. He pointed forward. "Look!" he whispered.

On the path before them were two deer, a buck and a doe, eating from a patch of mountain laurel. It was a wonderful sight.

"Is that one of Santa's reindeer?" shouted young Dick.

His excitement spooked the deer. Sensing the intrusion, the large buck extended its head into the air, his nose pointing to the sky. Then, in an instant, the buck dashed away, followed by the doe. They ran swiftly and with much grace to the bottom of the hill, where they vaulted the barbed-wire fence and disappeared over a ridge.

"Way to go, loudmouth!" Jule scolded.

Jule's comment set off a barrage of condemnation of young Dick's noisy reaction to seeing the deer.

"I'm sorry. I didn't mean to scare the deer away," young Dick said as he started to cry.

"Okay, okay, kids. Leave him alone," intervened Joseph. "He's just a baby. He didn't mean any harm."

Joseph lifted young Dick up on his shoulders and the excursion continued up the path, across a field, and down a ridge. They walked on and on, as Joseph began to tire.

"How many flapjacks did you eat for breakfast this morning?" Joseph kidded, looking up at his young son hoisted high on his shoulders.

"Just one."

"Well, it must have been an awfully big one, because you're getting pretty heavy," Joseph teased.

"Honest, Daddy, I just ate one," Dick answered, not knowing his father was joking.

"I guess you must be growing up on me then."

Joseph stopped to lighten his load. Gently placing Dick on the ground, he nudged him toward the sled. "Why don't you ride for a while and give your daddy a rest?"

"How much ... how much further?" Joseph asked Earl between breaths.

"It's just up over the ridge, Dad," Earl replied without turning around.

As they started up the steep grade, the resistance on the end of the rope attached to the sled suddenly became very heavy in Earl's hand. To a chorus of laughter, he finally turned around to discover that his father had replaced Dick and Boopie on the sled. Earl stopped.

"What are your doing, Dad?"

"I'm tired, so I thought I'd hop on for a ride up the hill," answered Joseph, his grin spread from ear to ear.

"Well, you'll have to get off because I can't pull you up that hill."

"You can't?" Joseph taunted. "I thought you were a tough guy. You mean to tell me that you can't pull your tired old dad up a little hill like that?"

"Well, I could, but I just don't want to."

"Betcha can't!"

Earl accepted his father's challenge, not at all confident in his own mind that he was up to the task. Off he went up the hill, his father in tow. Dick and Boopie walked close to Earl, hollering words of encouragement as he grunted with every step under the burdensome load. Elda and the girls walked behind giggling at the foolishness of the dare.

Earl's face glowed red as he struggled up the slope, his eyes squinting almost shut. Beads of sweat began to appear on his forehead as he neared the top of the crest. He was close to tasting victory. Joseph was equally close to tasting crow, but he wasn't about to let that happen. About ten yards from the top of the hill, Earl's momentum came to a sudden stop. He couldn't go any further. He turned around, and discovered that Joseph had been dragging his feet.

"No fair!" he protested, dropping the towrope.

"You lose!" Joseph laughed. He knew that Earl would have been successful, but he wouldn't give Earl the satisfaction of being able to brag.

Earl tossed a handful of snow at his father. A snow fight ensued and soon escalated into a full-blown wrestling match that sent Earl and Joseph tumbling, intertwined, down the hill. At the bottom, they both lay on their backs and laughed.

"Come on up here you fools!" shouted Elda, herself unable to stop laughing.

When Joseph reached the top of the hill, he noticed the stunning beauty of the place. He paused, taking a deep and reflective breath. A stand of tall, naked oak trees stood guard over the balsams, protecting them from the fierce wind that had begun to blow faint wispy clouds across the sky. The fragrance of balsam was everywhere. The branches of the fir trees were covered with pure white snow, giving the appearance that they wore coats of fleece. Their rich green color provided a warm contrast against the drab of white and gray in the forest. From where Joseph stood, he could see for miles. Looking down in the valley, he saw the township of Myersdale tucked into the mountains that extended as far as he could see.

Joseph put his arm around Earl's shoulder and looked over at his son.

Earl proudly walked over to a tree he had marked a few days earlier while hunting on the farm. "How about this one?" he said, grabbing the trunk and shaking it hard.

It was a tall tree with branches reaching outward some six feet across at the bottom. It was straight as an arrow and so full, hardly a speck of daylight could be seen through it. The group was quick to give its endorsement.

"That's a wonderful tree, son," said Joseph. "But before you cut it down, I think it would be a good idea if we said a little prayer of thanks." The Beals knelt around that magnificent fir and Joseph led them in humble prayer.

"Dear God, our Father in Heaven, we ask that you bless this majestic tree for our holiest of holidays, as we mark the birth of your Son, and our Savior, Jesus Christ. As we cut this tree and take it from its home among the God-filled glory of this scenic place, we ask that you fill us with your spirit of love and understanding. Thrust deep into our hearts and into our minds the true meaning of Christmas. Help us better understand the essence of what the birth of Jesus truly meant to mankind. Bless our family and our friends and all those on earth for now and evermore. Amen."

Earl retrieved the two-man saw from the sled and invited his father to help him cut down the tree.

"You and Boops do the honors. I'll sit here with your mother and watch."

Boopie, thrilled at the suggestion, quickly grabbed the saw from Earl and headed for the tree.

"Now, wait a minute there, Boopie," Earl chided as he yanked the saw from his brother's hand. "I'll get it started and call you when I need you. Now stand over there out of the way!"

Earl knelt by the tree and carefully guided the saw to the precise position where he wanted to begin his cut. The other children gathered around to watch.

Stepping forward and swiping his coat sleeve over his face to wipe his runny nose, Boopie anxiously asked, "Now?"

"Not yet. Stand back!" Earl answered impatiently, as he made the initial pass with the saw.

"Now?" Boopie asked again, as Earl began sliding the saw to and fro.

"Not yet!

Once Earl got the saw strokes gliding smoothly, he looked up at Boopie and reluctantly said to his overzealous helper, "Now!"

Boopie hastily grabbed the other end of the saw and, with great enthusiasm, began to push and pull out of cadence, working against Earl rather than with him.

"What are you trying to do, Boopie?" Earl asked, his annoyance apparent in his voice.

"I'm trying to help you cut the tree."

"Well then, pull when I push, and push when I pull!"

"What?"

"Like this," Earl demonstrated.

The children laughed at the comedy, but Boopie finally got

the hang of using the two-man saw.

Joseph and Elda sat and watched with amusement from their perch on a fallen oak tree that lay across the path. Joseph was touched by just how much this ritual meant to his children and how much fun they were having. He was glad he had decided to come along.

"This is a beautiful place, Elda."

"Yes, it is."

He turned, looked at her, and added, "And you're a beautiful woman."

Joseph put his arm around her. While he was holding her, she asked, "What made you change your mind?"

"I don't know. It's just a feeling I had. I can't explain it."

"I'm glad you did. It's nice having you here to share in this."

"I love you, Elda."

"I love you, too."

Their kiss was interrupted by a shout from Earl. "Okay, Dad, knock it off. We're finished here."

Joseph and Elda looked over to discover that the tree had been cut and lashed to the sled. There was now an audience of on-lookers sharing in their moment of tenderness.

It was time to head back. The sun was getting low in the sky and the temperature was dropping. The Beals began their descent off the mountain with their freshly cut Christmas tree.

Chapter VI

*T*he family huddled around the fire as it crackled and spit, radiating a warm, comfortable heat that was a welcome sensation after a day in the cold.

"Put on another log, Joseph. It's cold in here," Elda said. "I don't think my feet will ever be warm again."

"Yeah, but it sure was worth it. Just look at that tree," Earl said, bursting with pride as he stared through the window onto the back porch where the tree stood, propped up against the banister.

The other children crowded at the window, straining to get a better look.

"Can we bring it inside?" asked Dick.

"No, honey, we have to leave it outside for now. Santa will bring it in and decorate it on Christmas Eve like he always does," his mother replied.

"But it will get cold and lonely out there."

"Trees don't get lonely, silly," scoffed Jule.

"Yes they do! Mommy read me a story once about a tree that got lonely and cold, right, Mommy?" Dick insisted as he ran to his mother and climbed up on her lap.

"Yes, but that was a baby tree. Our Christmas tree is much older and stronger, and it will be just fine out on the porch," Elda reassured him with a smile.

The children resumed their places by the fire. But Anna remained at the window, staring at the tree. "How beautiful it is," she thought. "It's the most beautiful Christmas tree, ever. And, this tree is extra special because Daddy went with us to get it." Anna tried to imagine what the tree would look like when it was decorated with tinsel and glass balls.

"I'm starved. When do we eat?" asked Joseph, stroking his belly.

"Yea, that's what I was just about to say," Earl exclaimed.

Elda had become so comfortable by the fire that she had entirely forgotten about the evening meal.

"I'm sorry, I'll warm up some leftovers if that's alright?"

"That's fine with me. I'm so hungry I could eat anything," Earl answered. A budding young man, he was perpetually hungry.

Elda walked to the kitchen to begin preparing supper. Sis and Jule joined in to help her.

Joseph lay down on the sofa, figuring he'd use the time to take a quick nap or at least make an honest attempt. His eyes closed, and even though he was half asleep, he had the uncomfortable feeling that someone was watching him. He raised the lid of his right eye slightly and caught the image of Anna, standing over him, staring.

"What is it, Anna?"

"Nothing, Daddy."

He closed his eyes to resume his nap, but had the nagging sense that Anna was still standing there, staring at him. And she was.

"What?" He asked.

"Oh, I was just thinking."

"About what?"

"About you."

"What about me?"

"About how glad I am that you came with us today to get our Christmas tree."

Joseph sat up on the sofa and motioned for Anna to come over and sit next to him.

"Well, you know what?"

"What?"

"I'm glad I went too. I had a lot a fun today. Now I know what I've been missing all these years." He held her close to him.

❄ ❄ ❄

After supper the family adjourned to the living room where Joseph read, Elda knitted, and the children played. It was Saturday evening, which meant Earl could be found upstairs grooming himself for his date with Victoria Muller. Victoria was Earl's first love. She was about an inch taller than he, a fact which bothered her more than it did Earl. She was thin and long legged; her hair was chestnut brown and she had beautiful almond-shaped eyes. She and Earl had been classmates since the second grade. More recently, their relationship had blossomed into something more serious than playing dodge-ball and skipping stones on the river at the edge of town.

Suddenly, there was a reverberating roar coming from Earl's room.

"Boooooppppiiieeee! Get up here!"

All eyes in the living room focused on Boopie, knowing that Earl had undoubtedly uncovered some mischief done by the young prankster. The glee evident on Boopie's face confirmed their suspicion. From his expression, they could tell this one was a doozy, and it was.

"Boooooppppiiieeee! Where are you?"

Fearing the wrath of his older brother, Boopie jumped up and bolted from the room.

Earl stomped down the stairs and burst into the living room holding a mass of shoes, their laces all tied together in knots. A chorus of laughter greeted him. From Boopie's perspective, the caper was a success. He got the intended reaction from of his older brother, and the family was in stitches. And if Earl got his hands on Boopie, *he'd* probably be in stitches too!

"Where is that little …"

"Now, Now, Earl," Elda said in a protective way. "Settle down."

"Settle down? I'm late! Now I've got this to deal with. I can't go out with Victoria barefooted!"

"Here, give me your shoes. I'll untangle them. You go back upstairs and get ready. We'll deal with Boopie." Elda turned to Joseph and said, "You need to have a talk with our little joker."

"Boopie," Joseph called.

There was no answer.

"Boopie, if I have to get up and come looking for you…"

A muffled voice was heard coming from a secure hiding place under the stairs. "I'm coming, Daddy." Boopie, sensing that he might have gone too far this time, entered the living room with apprehension and cautiously approached his dad.

Joseph found it difficult to swallow his grin as he confronted his young son. "You need to stop this foolishness, young man," he said. "How would you like it if someone had done that to you?"

"I wouldn't care. Besides, I'll never have a date with a girl."

"You say that now, but you won't be saying that in a few years."

"Oh no. I don't even like girls."

"Well, I think you should apologize to Earl when he comes back downstairs."

"Do I have to?"

"Boopie!"

"Okay, Dad."

Earl came down to retrieve his shoes. As he sat on the sofa to put them on, Boopie plopped down next to him.

"Earl, are you mad at me?"

"Well, sort of, but I guess I'll get over it."

"Dad told me I have to tell you I'm sorry."

"Boopie!" growled Joseph.

"Well … I'm sorry, Earl."

"Apology accepted," Earl said as he finished lacing up his shoe.

Boopie leaned over and sniffed Earl's cheek several times.

"What's that funny smell? Do you have perfume on?" Boopie laughed.

Earl blushed, "Quiet, you little runt. I just splashed on a little of Dad's aftershave."

Boopie laughed again, looking around the room for support.

"What are you laughing about, Shrimp?

"Nothin', Earl. It's just ... never mind." Boopie was about to spout off another one of his annoying wisecracks, but he thought better of it, given the fact that he had just had his ears pinned back by his father for his fresh behavior. And, judging from the cold stare he was getting from Earl, he knew Earl had just about enough of his humor for the night.

"Well, I'll be off now," Earl announced to his parents. "I'm taking Victoria to the silent picture at the Main Street Theater. I won't be late."

❄ ❄ ❄

When Earl had gone, Anna walked over to Joseph and sat next to him. "Guess what, Daddy?"

"What?"

"I'm playing Mary in the church pageant on Christmas Eve."

"That's wonderful, honey."

"Will you be there to see me?"

"What time does it start?"

"Seven o'clock, I think," Elda answered.

"I hope I can be there. I'll try my best to get back in time." Joseph's job on the rails took him out of town many days. His schedule was often out of his control.

"Yeah, and I'm a wise man," Boopie bragged.

"Yes, you're a wise guy alright," Joseph laughed.

"Me too," said Dick, "I'm a wise guy in the play, too."

"How about you and Jule?" Joseph asked Sis.

"We're not actors, we're singers," she said proudly. "We're in the chorus, and I get to sing a solo."

"That's nice, sweetheart. I'm sure it will be a beautiful solo at that."

"Daddy?"

"What, Anna?"

"Can we set up the Nativity scene tonight?"

Joseph looked at Elda, who nodded her approval.

"Yes, I guess we can," he said.

"Oh goodie," Anna cried. While she and the other children accompanied their mother to the cellar to get the wooden crate that contained the Nativity set, Joseph cleared the table in the living room where the display was traditionally placed.

Excited, the children pulled open the crate and began grabbing for the pieces of the Nativity set.

"Careful, Boopie," warned Elda. "Those pieces are very fragile."

Anna was more subdued and careful in handling the items. Her face was radiant as she unwrapped the delicate figurines, which were securely bundled in rolls of paper. She paused when she came upon the figure of the baby Jesus. Holding it in the palm of her hand, she looked as though she had just discovered a hidden treasure.

She tried to imagine what it must have been like for Mary to hold Jesus the night he was born, so many years ago. For a moment, she pretended she was Mary. She pictured herself in the stable with Joseph and the animals. The wise men looked over her shoulder as she cuddled baby Jesus close to her. Her imagination got a bit out of hand, as the illusion took on a dimension of reality. The excitement caused her heart to accelerate and her palms to perspire. It was a powerful feeling.

"Anna … Anna!"

She had become lost in her fantasy and had not heard her father calling.

"I need to put baby Jesus in the crib."

Anna was clutching the glass figure of Jesus in her hand.

"Oh, okay, Daddy," she said as she snapped out of her daydream. She opened her hand to expose the glass ornament.

Joseph reached down and gently lifted the tiny statue from Anna's outstretched hand. Her eyes followed it as Joseph held up the ornament with admiration.

"This is what Christmas is all about, children - the Christ child," he said, as he gently laid the figure in the wooden manger.

Elda lit a candle and set it on the table to illuminate the scene. The children gathered around to listen as Joseph told them a story. Anna kept gazing at the Nativity all the while. After the story, and without looking away from the Nativity scene, she asked, "Can we sing some Christmas songs?"

"It's getting late, children. You have Sunday school tomorrow, so you must be getting to bed. Besides, you'll be singing plenty in church," Elda reminded them.

Joseph helped Elda get the children off to bed and both of them returned downstairs for some quiet time together. Elda put on the teakettle and joined Joseph at the kitchen table. She sat across from him. Clutching both of his hands, she gazed lovingly into his eyes.

"What are you looking at?"

"The most wonderful man alive," she said, smiling. "You made this day very special for me and the children."

"You know, I really enjoyed the day, too."

"And see, the world didn't come to an end because you came with us."

"Yeah, I guess you're right. Everything is still standing."

"I hope this becomes a tradition."

"We'll work on that," Joseph said with a wink and a grin.

They leaned over the table and began what was to be a long and tender kiss, but the teakettle would have none of it. The piercing blast of its whistle startled them apart. Ignoring the intrusion, they moved toward each other again and the instant their lips touched, they were again interrupted, this time by Boopie. He stood in the middle of the kitchen, three pajama top buttons undone, and his blond hair tangled and knotted.

"I can't sleep. What's that whistling noise?" he asked, rubbing his eyes and yawning.

"It's just the teakettle. Now go back to bed!" Joseph and Elda said in unison.

They looked at each other and laughed aloud. Six children and a job on the railroad left them with too few private moments together. After a cup of tea and a few sugar cookies, Elda and Joseph decided to turn in. It had been a long day, and they were tired.

❄ ❄ ❄

In the middle of the night, a voice awakened Joseph and Elda.

"Daddy, Daddy!" Anna cried out.

"I'll go see what's wrong," Joseph said as he climbed out of bed and rushed to Anna's room to calm her.

"What's wrong, angel?"

"I'm scared."

"Of what?"

"I had a bad dream."

"What did you dream about, honey?"

"Jesus … He was holding out his hand and asking me to give him my ring - the one you and mommy gave me for my birthday. I'm scared, Daddy!"

"You need not be afraid of Jesus. He won't hurt you. And besides, honey, it was only a dream. Now go back to sleep, sweet heart."

Joseph stayed with her, lightly stroking her forehead until she fell asleep.

"What was it?" Elda asked upon his return.

"Anna was having a dream."

"About what?"

"Oh nothing, dear, I'll tell you in the morning. Now let's get some sleep."

But Joseph lay awake, trying to determine what was behind these dreams of Jesus and references to rings. He might have dismissed his own dream as an inconsequential vision in the night, but Anna's too? It was so similar to his. This must to be more than a coincidence, he thought.

Eventually, Joseph dozed off. During the night, the music returned. The dream and the bright image of Jesus twice visited him. In each dream, the same faint melody played as Jesus held out his hand and said, "Joseph, take this gift from me to you as a token of my love. It was a gift of gold given to me by one of the wise men at the manger the night I was born in Bethlehem. It does me no good, yet it will bring others great joy."

In the previous dreams, Joseph always woke up as he reached for the ring. But tonight, in the second vision, Joseph held out his hand, and Jesus placed a small golden ring into his palm. Then he disappeared. Holding the ring, Joseph felt a curious warmth radiating from it. The heat passed through his body. It was a strange sensation, almost euphoric.

He looked down at the ring, which was glowing gloriously in his hand. It was ravishing. The gold was luminous and a small red ruby was set in the elaborately carved face. The ruby glistened brilliantly in the light, almost hypnotizing Joseph as he stared at it. Then, he awakened, and it was gone.

"What is it, Joseph?" Elda asked. "You're trembling."

"Oh, just a dream. Just a dream."

"This certainly is a night for dreams."

"Seems that way, doesn't it."

"Good night, honey."

"Good night."

Chapter VII

"Hold still, Anna," Jule said, making the final adjustments to the red ribbon she just placed in Anna's hair. "I need to use the mirror too, Sis," she complained, turning to her big sister. "You've been hogging it all morning!"

"I just can't get my hair to curl right in the back. Can you help me?" Sis asked.

"Your hair looks fine. Now move over!"

Sunday mornings always began with a tumultuous uproar more indicative of a free-for-all than a family preparing for church. The chatter that leaked through the bathroom door was nonstop, intermixed with giggles, squeals, and bantering, as the three sisters, completely self-absorbed, monopolized the bathroom while they primped.

"There's a cute new boy in Sunday school class," Sis told her sisters.

"What's his name?" Asked Jule.

"I don't know, but I aim to find out today."

"Hurry up, girls, your father needs to get into the bathroom to shave," their mother yelled up the stairs.

Elda had the overwhelming task of orchestrating the family's on-time arrival for the morning service. This was a responsibility of immense proportions. Having three girls in the house added measurably to the preparation time needed when going anywhere that required dressing up.

"Okay, Mom, we'll be out in a minute," Sis replied.

As Elda dried the last glass from the breakfast dishes, she felt a tug on the back of her dress. She looked down to discover young Dick with an expression of great urgency looming on his face.

"Mommy, I have to go to the bathroom."

"Okay, honey. The girls will be finished in a few minutes and Boopie can take you upstairs to go."

"But I ... I have to go real bad."

"Alright," she said. "Boopie ... Boopie? ... Boopie!" Elda's calls went unanswered. She happened to glance out the kitchen window and was forced to do a double take. There in the back-yard was Boopie, in his best Sunday clothes, on his knees in the snow, having a snowball battle with the neighbor boys, his canine companion, Nelly, at his side.

Elda went to the door and reprimanded him, ordering him inside.

From behind she heard, "Mommy, I have to go to the bathroom *reeeeeaaaaallll* bad!" Dick was jumping up and down with his legs crossed.

She took him by the hand and led him up the stairs to the bathroom door. Her knock shook the door on its hinges. The giggling inside stopped.

"Out of the bathroom ... now!"

The door swung open and there was a mass exodus: first Sis, then Jule and Anna. Joseph stuck his head out of his bedroom door to see if the bathroom was vacant yet. Elda handed off Dick to Joseph and retreated back downstairs to deal with

Boopie.

"Boopie!" The knees of his pants were wet and soiled with mud. "Get upstairs and change your pants. And be quick about it," she scolded.

About that time, there was another impending emergency. Anna came running into the kitchen, hysterical.

"My ring! My ring! I've lost my ring. I can't find it anywhere!"

"Settle down, Anna. We'll find it. Do you remember where you were when you took it off?"

"I can't remember. I can't!" she sobbed. "What am I going to do? I've lost it!"

"Did you have it when we came back from cutting the Christmas tree?" her mother asked.

"I think so," she paused. "I don't remember. Maybe I lost it when I took my gloves off to play in the snow," she said as she burst into tears again.

"Oh, Anna. How could you be so careless? That ring was expensive. It cost your mommy and daddy a lot of money."

The ring was Anna's most prized possession. She wore it everywhere. It had been a gift from her mother and father for her ninth birthday, a gift that had enormous meaning to her. She had always wanted a ring like it.

Elda took Anna upstairs and enlisted the aid of her sisters to search for the ring. They looked everywhere - under the beds, in the closets, in Anna's bed covers, in the hallway, along the stairs, everywhere, but despite the exhaustive search, Anna's precious ring did not turn up. Anna was frantic.

With a collective gasp, the group concluded, "The bathroom!" At that exact moment, Joseph, completely unaware of the calamity outside, emerged from the bathroom having completed his shave. As he opened the door, he was greeted by the search mob.

"What's the attraction?" he said. Holding up Anna's ring between his index finger and thumb, he casually observed, "Anna, I found your ring on the bathroom sink. You must have taken it off to wash your hands and forgotten to put it back on."

"Oh, Daddy! You found it! Thank you! You're my hero!" Anna said, clinging to his waist.

Joseph looked a bit surprised at Anna's elation. He had merely picked up her ring from the bathroom sink, and had become an instant hero. But he was quick to accept the title. He looked over at Elda, who was standing there, wearing a frazzled look on her face, hands on her hips, shaking her head at him and smiling.

"Yeah. Daddy's a real hero, alright," she said. "He looked everywhere for that darn ring before it popped up in front of him."

Anna was relieved. She slid the ring back on her finger and said, "I'll never take this ring off again, Daddy."

"Well, let's break up this happy little gathering. We need to hurry up if we're going to get to church on time," Elda said, sending everyone scattering.

Feeling overwhelmed, she slouched down on the chair that sat below the window in the upstairs hallway. She took a deep breath and exhaled loudly as she placed both hands on her forehead in exhausted frustration. She ran the fingers of both hands through her hair. As they came to rest at the base of her neck, she clasped them together and looked up at the ceiling. Smiling, she said, "Oh, God, please give me strength." Then she took another deep breath and stood up to resume the battle. Eventually, she won.

❄ ❄ ❄

Elda held the front door open, and one by one, the children filed past her onto the porch. Joseph took up the rear, closing the door behind him. Finally, they were off to church.

Myersdale was a tight-knit community and religious by nature. Churches marked many of the corners in the picturesque hamlet. The Beals worshiped at Myersdale Lutheran, only a few doors up from their house on North Street.

The church had been built in the early 1800s. It was huge, and made from gray stone. It had an impressive, if not intimidating, bell tower that rose high above the town. And when the bells rang, the ground at the base of the tower trembled. At the very top of the steeple was a white cross that could be seen for miles. Inside, the gray stone walls made the chapel seem cold when it was empty. But on Sundays, if one arrived late, seating was hard to find. When the choir sang, when the massive organ played, and when the sunlight filtered through the elegant stained-glass windows, the solid stone church was a very warm place to be.

The Beals went to church regularly, every Sunday, except for Joseph, who had to work most Sundays. This was one of the things he disliked most about his job. He was looking forward to going to church today. It had been several months since he had the opportunity to worship on a Sunday. Most of the time, he went to the church and worshiped in private on his day off.

It was a dreary day with winter storm clouds threatening. As the Beals walked up North Street to church, large flakes of snow fell like feathers from above.

Reverend Ernest Twigg greeted the family at the door. Ernest was a no-nonsense type of minister who didn't mince words - just told it like it was. He was a rugged man; a man's man. That was one reason why Joseph liked him so much. He gave fiery sermons from deep within his heart. He rarely prepared a sermon ahead of time. He just went to the altar and talked about whatever moved him at the moment. Ernest Twigg was a popular man in town and had been pastor of Myersdale Lutheran for close to twenty years.

"Good morning and Merry Christmas to you all."

"Good morning, Reverend," Joseph said as he shook the pastor's hand.

"It's good to have you with us this Sunday, Joseph."

"It's great to be here among these good people."

Joseph led his family through the imposing wooden doors, and they found their seats in the front of the church. He always liked to sit in the same place: first pew, left-hand side, on the end. He had more leg room there and didn't feel so confined. Besides, it was almost always available; for some reason, the first pew was always the last to be filled.

Joseph turned to Elda and asked, "Is Earl coming?"

"Yes. He said he was going to pick up Victoria and walk her to church this morning."

The organ began to play, and the congregation rose to sing the first hymn. Joseph started singing. His baritone voice could be heard several rows away. He sang a bit off key, but to him it sounded just fine. Those around him, fortunately, had a forgiving nature. As he bellowed out the anthem, he looked around, impatiently for Earl. His eyes darted from left to right, his large neck craned over the rows behind him. Then, through the back door, Earl appeared. Snow covered his hair as he ushered his young lady through the crowd that was still standing at the back of the church. Joseph signaled for them to join him and the family in their pew.

Earl and Victoria arrived at their seats just as the hymn was ending. Joseph looked sternly at Earl, who clearly sensed his father's irritation regarding his tardiness. As if confronting an angry dog, Earl tried to avoid direct eye contact with his father.

When the service was over, Joseph and Elda joined the congregation in the church cellar for some fresh-baked pastries and coffee during the social hour. The children went off to Sunday school.

After exchanging the season's greetings with their fellow parishioners, Joseph and Elda left the church and returned home. They strolled arm in arm down North Street, while the dark winter sky lazily spit large flakes of snow.

"I meant to ask you about Anna's dream last night," Elda said.

"She had this strange dream about Jesus. He was holding his hand out to her, asking her to give him her ring. I guess it scared her a little."

"What about your dream? You were shaking when you woke

73

up in the middle of the night."

"It's the strangest thing."

"What?"

"My dream was about Jesus, too. Only in my dream, he was trying to give me a ring."

"That is strange that both of you would have similar dreams. Perhaps setting up the Nativity scene last night made you and Anna dream about Jesus."

"Could be. But what is this business about rings? I don't understand it. And this isn't the first time I had such a dream. I had the same dream on Friday night."

"Well, what do you think it is?"

"I don't know, Elda, it puzzles me."

Once home, Joseph, tired from the uneasy night, lay down for a quick nap. Elda began preparing the Sunday meal. Before long, Earl returned home from Sunday school with Dick and Boopie.

"Where are the girls?" Elda asked.

"They walked downtown with some of their friends to look in the shop windows. They said they wouldn't be long."

"But it's so cold out, Earl. Why didn't you tell them to come straight home?"

"They're bundled up fine, Mom. They'll be alright."

Chapter VIII

A snowball landed about four feet from the group of girls gathered in front of McNichol's General Store. A chorus of giggles erupted as Sis chanted, "You missed us, You missed us," to the gang of boys assembled across the street.

"Isn't that the new boy in our Sunday school class, Sis?" Mary cried. Mary Higgins was Sis's best friend. Both of them had a crush on this new boy in town.

"Oh, yes. Isn't he the cutest?" Sis said, giggling.

"What's his name?" asked Jule, batting her eyes as if to mock her older sister.

"Tommy Madden," snapped Sis. "And forget it. He's too old for you!"

In another show of immature flirtation, the young boys lobbed a few more snowballs across the street, causing the girls to dodge and giggle some more. Then the band of adolescent romeos ran, laughing, down the street and out of sight.

Anna and her sisters were fascinated by the Christmas displays in the store windows. The local merchants took great pride in their holiday decorating, one always trying to outdo the other. In McNichol's General Store window, there was a life-size sleigh, complete with Santa and three elves. Not to be outdone, O'Grady's Feed and Seed had a real reindeer in a makeshift corral in the alley near the loading docks. And,

Murphy's Dry Goods had a most realistic looking Nativity scene.

"Look at that Santa. He looks so real!" Anna said to her friend, Catherine Brown.

"I can't wait until Christmas," Catherine said. "Santa is going to bring me so many toys. I just know he is." She spouted off a long list of the things she wanted, and then turned to Anna and said, "What do you want Santa to bring you?"

Anna pondered for a minute, then in a gracious voice said, "I'd like a new baby doll and some doll clothes, but, whatever Santa decides to bring is okay with me."

"Let's go over and feed the reindeer at O'Grady's," shouted Jule. The idea received favor from the gathering and the girls ran to the alley behind the feed store.

The reindeer was lying down at the back of the corral. It took quite a bit of coaxing from the girls to get him up on his feet and over to the front of the pen so they could get a better look at him. Once there, he sniffed their hands curiously, searching for something to eat.

They were all somewhat cautious, even a bit afraid of this unfamiliar, yet gentle creature. He startled them when he snorted, blowing steam from his nostrils. The girls screamed in harmony and retreated a few yards before realizing they had nothing to fear from this beautiful animal.

Anna pulled a piece of maple candy from her coat pocket and held it up to the fence. The reindeer smelled the candy, then began to lick it, while Anna held it in her hand.

"Look, he likes it!" Anna said with excitement.

The reindeer pulled the candy from Anna's grasp; it fell to

the ground and he devoured it.

Sis nudged Anna and said, "Come on. We ought to be going home. Mom will be worried about us."

The group wended its way down the street, stopping occasionally to admire some decorations or to participate in an impromptu snowball fight. As they passed Murphy's Dry Goods Store, Anna stopped to study the Nativity scene in the store window. The group continued down the street without her, completely unaware that she had stopped.

Anna looked at the pleasant expression on Mary's face. "How beautiful she is," Anna thought. Then she looked at the baby Jesus, lying in the manger, angels hovering above him. Her heart began to race as she stared at the Christ child through the window. She remembered the dream that frightened her from her sleep the night before, the dream where Jesus held out his hand and asked for her ring. Anna slipped the glove from her right hand and stared down at her ring. She replayed the dream in her head. Then, she turned her gaze back to the wooden Christ child.

"Anna! Anna!" yelled Sis. "Come on, we have to go home!"

Sis's call surprised her, causing her to jump. Anna's eyes refocused from the Christ child to her own reflection in the store window. She stood there looking at herself, not knowing what to think. She was afraid and confused. Suddenly, something tugged at her arm. She screamed!

"Anna! What's wrong with you?" It was Sis. "Come on, we've got to go!"

Sis and Anna caught up with the group and continued down Main Street. At the corner, they split up, as Sis, Jule, and Anna turned on North Street and walked toward their house. Anna stopped to pet a stray cat. She always had a soft spot for stray animals. When she started to walk away, the cat followed. She stopped, picked it up, and put it inside her coat to keep it warm. She could hear it purr as it rubbed its head against her chin while she walked.

Anna hurried to catch up to her sisters. When she passed the small park a few blocks from her house, she noticed a little girl about her age sitting on a bench. The girl's face was soiled and her cheeks were streaked with tears. She wore a tattered coat and her gloves were full of holes. As Anna passed her, she could hear the girl crying.

❄ ❄ ❄

Elda heard the giggles of her daughters coming from the back yard. She looked out the kitchen window and saw Jule and Sis fixing the snowman's nose and placing a few lumps of coal on his chest to serve as buttons for his coat of white.

She opened the kitchen door and walked out onto the back porch. Folding her arms across her chest to keep warm she said, "Come in and change your clothes and take off your good coats before you go back out to play." Then she noticed the absence of Anna.

"Where's Anna?"

"She'll be along in a while," said Sis. "She stopped to talk to a little girl up the street."

Elda went back inside and resumed her cooking, watching through the window for Anna.

❄ ❄ ❄

"What's the matter? Why are you crying?" Anna asked the little girl in a concerned voice.

The girl didn't answer. Anna's attention made her weep even more openly. Anna put the cat down and sat next to the girl on the bench. Putting her arm around her, Anna again asked the little girl what was wrong.

"Nothin'," she answered defiantly, staring straight ahead.

Not knowing what else to say, Anna tried, "My name's Anna. What's yours?"

The girl was apprehensive.

"What's your name?" Anna asked again.

"Martha. Martha Shultz," the girl snapped.

"Martha. That's a pretty name," Anna said. "So what's wrong, Martha? Why are you crying?"

"Well … it's … well … everything's wrong," the girl sighed. "My daddy's lost his job. We have no money, no place to live, and I'm so cold and hungry," the girl said as she sniffed back her tears.

"I've never seen you before. You don't live around here, do you?"

"No. We're from Elk Lick. We're just passing through, headed for Cumberland where my daddy says he can find work."

"Where's your mommy and daddy?"

"Over there," Martha said, as she pointing across the street. Anna saw a wagon hitched to two scraggly-looking workhorses, their rib cages clearly visible through their brown shaggy coats. A man labored frantically, trying to fix a rear wheel that sat askew. Beside him stood a frail woman holding an infant bundled in her arms.

"Our wagon's broke. My daddy's trying to fix it, but he needs help."

Anna looked across the street and saw, Reverend Twigg and his wife, Gladys, walking with Richard and Eleanor Wahl. She grabbed Martha by the hand and pulled her over to where Reverend Twigg and his group were walking.

"Reverend Twigg! Reverend Twigg!" Anna shouted.

"What is it, Anna?"

"This is Martha," she said, pointing to her new friend. "Her mommy and daddy are over there. Their wagon's broke and they need help."

The group approached the man struggling with the wagon wheel. As they neared, he looked up. The look on his face was one of desperation, an expression that was mirrored by his wife, who stood shivering as she cradled the sleeping baby in her arms.

Reverend Twigg, smiling, extended his right hand. The man stood to shake it. Introducing himself, Ernest said, "Looks like you're having a bit of trouble here. Can we lend you a hand?"

The man's despair was lightened somewhat by Ernest Twigg's smile of hope. "Thank you, sir. I sure could use some help. My name is Frank Shultz. This is my wife, Rebecca, and that's my daughter, Martha."

"Yes, we've met, haven't we, Martha?" Reverend Twigg said with a wink. "This is my wife, Gladys, and my friends, Richard and Eleanor Wahl."

"Daddy, this is my new friend, Anna. She stopped to help me and brought these people to help you," Martha told her father.

Martha's father rubbed Anna on the head. "Thank you, Anna, for your concern."

"Oh, you're welcome, sir."

"We were heading to Cumberland from Elk Lick. I was hoping to make it there by tonight, but my wagon broke down."

The man proceeded to tell the group of his predicament, about losing his job and his home. "I hear there's work in Cumberland."

"Gladys, why don't you and Eleanor take Rebecca, the baby, and Martha back to our house so they can get warm. Richard and I will help Frank get this wagon fixed, and then we'll all be along to get something to eat."

"That's so kind of you, sir," said Rebecca.

"Why don't you and your family spend the night with us and leave for Cumberland in the morning?" Gladys offered.

"Oh, we couldn't impose on you in such a way," Frank answered.

"Don't you worry about imposing. We insist that you stay," barked Ernest. "It would be foolish for you to try to make it to Cumberland tonight. Besides, you have no place to stay there, anyway. Spend the night with us, get a good night's sleep, and leave tomorrow." Patting one of the horses on the rump, Ernest continued, "We'll take these horses over to O'Grady's and get them fed. It looks like it's been a long time between meals."

"Unfortunately, it has been, sir. It's all I can do to feed my family. Sometimes my horses have to go without."

"Momma, can I stay and play with Anna while Reverend Twigg and Mr. Wahl help Daddy fix the wagon?"

"I suppose that will be alright," Rebecca replied.

While the men worked on the wagon, Anna and Martha ran back to the park to play.

"Gee, that's a perfect snow angel, Martha!"

"Yours is pretty good, too, Anna."

"Yeah, except for the crooked wings," Anna laughed.

As the two of them stood, admiring their work, Martha asked, "Do you believe in angels?"

"Yep. I sure do," Anna replied. "My mommy says each of us has an angel who looks after us."

"The day we lost our house, my momma said our angel must have taken a vacation."

"Where do you sleep at night, if you don't have a house," Anna asked.

"Oh … here and there," Martha said. "We stayed with my aunt for a while. We've slept in churches, in kind strangers' homes. It's not so bad," Martha said, trying to put on the best face that she could. "Daddy says things will get better once we get to Cumberland."

"Well, if you keep moving around, how is Santa going to find you to bring you your presents?" Anna asked.

"I don't know," answered Martha, looking down. "He couldn't find me last year either."

"Hey! I've got a great idea!" Anna smiled, attempting to cheer Martha up. "Let's build a snowman!"

Anna and Martha giggled as they labored to roll a large ball of snow for the base of their snowman. When the mass of snow got too heavy to roll any further, they stopped to rest, sitting in the snow, their backs resting against the huge snowball. Martha heard her father call out to her.

"Martha. We're all finished. Say good-bye to your friend and come along. We must go."

"Oh, Daddy, we were just going to make a snowman."

"We can't keep these good people waiting. Now come along."

"Okay, Daddy. I'm coming."

Anna and her new friend hated to say good-bye. After all, it was just a short while ago that they said hello.

Martha reached out and held Anna's hands. "Gee, I wish you could be my friend always, and that we could play together everyday."

"Me too," Anna said as she looked down at the poor girl's fingers sticking out of the holes in her gloves. She felt sorry for her.

"Your fingers must get awfully cold."

"Yeah, sometimes. When they do, I just put them in my coat pockets, and that usually warms them up."

Anna thought back to the Sunday school lesson she learned earlier in the day about the joy of giving. She had learned that it was more blessed to give than to receive. She thought about this poor little girl and her family's spell of bad fortune. She couldn't image what it would be like not to have a home. She wanted to help, but didn't know what she could do.

"Here," Anna said as she squirmed her fingers free from her gloves. "You take my gloves. They'll keep your hands warm."

"But ... but, they're like new," Martha said as she examined them.

"That's okay. I have two more pairs at home."

"Oh, thank you, Anna. You're so nice."

Martha noticed Anna's ring, exposed on her bare hand.

"That's a very pretty ring."

"Yeah," Anna said, holding up her hand to look at the ring. "My mommy and daddy gave me this ring for my birthday. It's my favorite thing in the whole world. It has special powers, too." she exaggerated.

"Like what?"

"It keeps me safe. It's my good luck charm."

"Wow," Martha said with astonishment.

Anna wished she could do more to help Martha and her family. She wished she could spend more time with her new friend. But, it was time for them to say good-bye. They embraced each other until Martha's father called out again.

"Come on, Martha, we have to go!"

Martha began to slowly walk toward her father and Ann shouted, "Good-bye, Martha."

Martha walked a few steps, then stopped and turned around.

"I'll miss you," she said to Anna.

"I'll miss you, too."

Anna stood in the park and watched as Martha and her father, Reverend Twigg, and Mr. Wahl climbed aboard the wagon. Martha's father gave a whistle and made a clicking sound with this tongue against his cheek, signaling the horses to begin their pull. The wagon turned in front of Anna and headed down the street to the Twiggs' house. Anna and Martha waved their final good-byes.

❄ ❄ ❄

Elda looked out the kitchen window and watched her children playing in the snow. There was still no sign of Anna. It was odd for her to be so late and Elda was beginning to wonder if something had happened to her. She was just about to put on her coat and go searching when she saw Anna walk through the backyard and up the steps onto the porch.

"Where have you been, little girl? I was worried about you," Elda asked when Anna opened the door.

"I stopped to talk to a girl in the park."

"You should have come home with your sisters and changed your clothes before you went out to play."

"Sorry, Mom."

"Who did you stop to talk to?"

"A girl named Martha Shultz."

"I've never heard you talk about her before."

"Oh, she's not from around here. She's from Elk Lick, just passing through with her family on the way to Cumberland."

"Cumberland? That's a long way."

"Yeah. Her daddy's out of work. They lost their home and her daddy's going to try to get a job there."

"What was the little girl doing in the park?" asked Elda.

"Her daddy's wagon broke. I fetched Reverend Twigg and Mr. Wahl to help him fix it. The Twiggs invited them to supper and to spend the night."

"That was nice of the Reverend and Mrs. Twigg to put them up."

"Yeah, Martha was pretty sad. She was crying. She said they didn't have any food or any money."

"I'm sure Reverend Twigg will see that they are provided

for," Elda said. "By the way, where are your gloves, child?"

Fearing she might be in trouble, Anna cautiously answered, "Well … ah … Martha's gloves were … um … full of holes, Mommy. She was cold, so … so I gave her mine. Besides, I have two more pairs. She didn't have any without holes in them, Mommy, and …"

Elda looked down at Anna and smiled. "That was a very nice thing you did, Anna. I'm proud of you."

"Mommy?"

"Yes."

"If Martha doesn't have a home and is traveling around, how will Santa find her?"

"Oh, I'm sure he will. Santa is a pretty smart fellow."

"But she said he couldn't find her last year."

Elda now realized that the family was too poor even to buy gifts for their children. "Does Martha have any brothers or sisters?" she asked.

"Yeah. She has a brother, but he's just a baby."

"Well, maybe he missed her last year, but I have a feeling ol' Santa will find Martha this year," Anna's mother reassured her. In her heart, however, Elda knew that the likelihood of Santa finding Martha this year was slim. But she had a plan.

"After supper, can I go over to the Twiggs' to see Martha again?" Anna asked.

"We'll see. Now why don't you run along up stairs and change your clothes."

Anna flew by her father as he was entering the kitchen. "Hi, Daddy!" she screamed as she ran past him.

"Anna sure seems excited," Joseph remarked.

"Yes, she's feeling pretty good right now," Elda said. She told Joseph about the new friend Anna met in the park. She told him of the girl's plight and how Anna had given her gloves to the little girl.

"Isn't that just like our Anna?" Joseph smiled

Elda walked over to him and gave him a gentle hug.

"It sure is."

"I was thinking, Joseph," Elda said. "I have a few extra gifts I got for the girls that I'd like to wrap up and send over to the Twiggs' for Anna's friend, Martha. I think that's what I'll do."

Earl trotted downstairs yelling, "Mom!"

"I'm in the kitchen."

He burst into the room, "Mom, Victoria's family invited me over to spend the afternoon and to stay for supper. Is it alright?"

Elda looked at Joseph for his reaction. Receiving none, she said, "I guess it's okay. Just don't be too late coming home."

"Thanks, Mom. See you later, Dad!" Earl said as he shot from the room. It wasn't but a second later that the front door slammed as he bolted up the street.

"Ahhhhh, ain't young love great?" Joseph smiled.

"Yes, but old love isn't too bad either," Elda said as she gave Joseph a peck on the lips and whirled around to attend to something cooking in the oven. She bent over and opened the oven door, allowing a delicious aroma to escape.

Joseph's nose caught a whiff of a sweet smell. "What's that?" he asked. "It smells good. Smells like..."

"Banana bread," Elda interrupted. She turned around with her back to the stove, putting her hands on her hips in a defensive stance. "Don't be hovering around the oven like a vulture," she said, smiling. "It won't be done for a while yet."

"Oh, Elda," Joseph said as he stepped forward, playfully grabbing her by the waist. "You make the best banana bread this side of the Mississippi."

"Your flattery will get you nowhere," she grinned, pushing him away.

"Can't I just sneak a little taste?" Joseph kidded.

"No! Now go!" she said smiling, pointing her finger in the direction of the living room.

Elda went down to the cellar to get a few toys that Santa had hidden there, toys that he was to put under the Beals' tree on Christmas Eve. "Surely the children won't miss them," she thought. There were still plenty of toys left to make her children's Christmas special. She knew she needed to help Santa find Martha, so she selected a few toys that she hoped would bring joy to the little girl on Christmas morning.

Elda brought the presents upstairs and wrapped them on a table in the pantry. On the gift tags, she wrote, "To Martha, with love, from Santa." Then she put the packages in a bag and hid the bag behind some boxes in the pantry.

Chapter IX

Upstairs, Anna hurried to get out of her Sunday clothes. She had such a good feeling in her heart for what she had done and for the praise her mother had given her. She couldn't stop thinking about Martha, though. She talked about Martha to her secret friend, Teddy, a tattered stuffed teddy bear she had since she was three. Teddy was the special friend she could trust with secrets. Anna could tell Teddy anything, and her secret would be safe.

"Teddy, I feel sorry for Martha," she said. "She doesn't have a home, and Santa won't be able to find her. Her mommy and daddy are poor and they can't buy food. How will they eat? Where will they live for Christmas, Teddy? What if Martha's daddy can't find a new job in Cumberland? What will they do then?" Teddy was a good listener. Sometimes, he even talked to Anna, but only she could hear his voice.

Anna's mood changed quickly. Her feelings of goodness and hope faded as she thought more about her new friend's situation.

"What can I do to help Martha, Teddy? I gave her my gloves, but what else can I do to help her family have a nice Christmas?"

Folding her hands in her lap, she looked down at her ring. She reflected back upon her Sunday school lesson and what

Mrs. Olson, her Sunday school teacher, told the class about giving.

"Mrs. Olson said it was good to be generous, Teddy, especially to poor people." Anna had learned many lessons about giving during the past few weeks at Sunday school. The week before, she had to memorize a verse from Proverbs about giving and recite it before her class: "He that giveth unto the poor shall not lack: but he that hideth his eyes shall have many a curse."

She slipped the ring off her finger and examined it more closely. She recalled the scary dream she had the night before, when Jesus appeared and asked her to give Him her ring. She held the ring up, showing it to Teddy.

"This morning when I lost this, Mommy said it cost a lot of money. Maybe I could give it to Martha and her daddy could sell it, and get money for it."

Teddy thought this was an excellent idea, but Anna still wasn't quite sure.

"But, I really like this ring, Teddy. It's my good luck charm. It makes me feel safe when I wear it," she said. "I'd really miss it if I gave it away."

Anna wondered if she was being selfish. She looked around the room at all the things she had. Martha had nothing; she didn't even have a Teddy.

"You're right, Teddy. I should give her my ring. That's what I'll do!" Anna raced out of the room, ran down the stairs, grabbed her coat and hat, and joined her brothers and sisters in the backyard for a few minutes of frolic in the snow before supper. All the while playing, Anna couldn't help thinking about her decision to part with her ring. She was experiencing conflict. She wanted to help Martha, but she really liked her ring and she was having second thoughts.

"Time for supper, kids," Elda called from the back door. Anna liked the feeling she got when she came in from the cold after playing in the snow. The kitchen was such a warm and cozy place. And today was extra special, because they were having roasted chicken and mashed potatoes with gravy, Anna's favorite. During supper, Elda told the family about Anna's good deed.

"That was very thoughtful of you, Anna," said Joseph.

"Thank you, Daddy," she said as she sat a little taller in her chair.

"Mommy, when I'm through with supper can I go over to the Twiggs' for a little while to see Martha once more?" Anna asked.

"For a little while. But you have to help your sisters clean up the dishes first."

"Oh, goodie!" she squealed.

While Anna and her sisters cleaned up the dishes from the table, Elda brought the bag of toys from the pantry and placed it just outside the back door on the porch. Anna finished helping her sisters and asked, "Can I go now, Mommy?"

"Yes, but I want you home by seven thirty."

"But we don't have school tomorrow."

"Seven thirty, Anna."

"Okay, Mommy."

Anna buttoned up her coat and opened the back door to leave.

"Mommy! There's a bag of presents on the back porch."

"What?" Elda said with pretend surprise, as she looked at Joseph and winked.

"Yes!" Anna shouted. "He found her! Santa found Martha! He brought her presents to our house!"

Anna was so happy. She was jumping up and down with joy.

"I'll take them to her, Mommy. She'll be so happy."

"That's a pretty heavy load for a little girl to carry. How 'bout if I carry the bag of packages for you," said Joseph. "I could use a good walk and some fresh air, anyway."

"That's a good idea, Daddy. Can we go now?"

"Hold on a minute. Let me get my coat."

Joseph held Anna's hand as they walked down the sidewalk. It was a crisp evening. Their breath quickly turned to a frozen mist when it hit the cold air. The snow on the sidewalk crunched under their feet as they walked. The sky was clear and the stars were abundant. Joseph stopped and knelt down next to Anna. Pointing up to the sky he said, "Just look at all those stars. Aren't they beautiful?"

"Yeah, and there sure is a lot of them, too."

"See that?" Joseph said, pointing to cluster of stars. "That's the Big Dipper."

"Where, Daddy?"

"There. Can't you see the shape the stars make?" he said, tracing the outline against the sky with his finger. "Doesn't it look like the dipper we used to scoop the water out of the spring on Saunders farm last summer?"

"Oh, Yeah, now I see it!"

"And over there, that's the Little Dipper."

"What's that big, bright star, Daddy?"

"That's the North Star, honey, the brightest star in the sky."

"It looks like the star the three wise men followed to baby Jesus."

"Yes, it does. But that was a very special star, Anna, and much brighter."

"Oh, Daddy. Look at that! A shooting star!"

"They say when you see a shooting star, you should make a wish."

"If I do, will my wish come true?"

"It may."

Anna closed her eyes. She knew what she was going to wish for. She wished for Martha to have a very special Christmas.

"Well, my little angel, we better be running along, or it will be time for you to come home before you even get to where you're going."

As they walked, Anna again thought about her ring, and whether she should give it to Martha.

"Daddy?"

"What, Anna?"

"If you had something that you really liked a lot and somebody else needed it, would you give it to them?"

"Well ... that depends."

"On what?"

"On what it was, and how much the person needed it. Why?"

"Oh, I was just wondering. But what if it was something you really liked?"

"Well, I suppose, if I really liked the person a lot and they really needed what I had ... well, I suppose I would give it to them. You know, the Bible says, 'Give and it shall be given unto you.' God doesn't want you to give things grudgingly."

"What's grudgingly mean?"

"It means … when you don't really want to give something, or you feel you must, but you don't really want to. God wants people to be unselfish and to give freely to others in need. God loves a cheerful giver."

"He does?"

"Yes, he sure does. What's this all about, anyway?"

"Oh nothing, I was just thinking about what we learned in Sunday school today."

Joseph, unknowingly, had just talked Anna right out of her ring. His remarks confirmed her decision to give it to Martha. Anna had an easier feeling about it now.

Joseph knocked on the door and Gladys Twigg answered.

"Good evening. What a nice surprise, come on in."

"Oh, I can't stay, Gladys. I just carried these packages down for Anna."

"Packages?"

"Yeah, Santa left these presents for Martha at my house!" Anna shouted.

"Oh my! That will surely be a nice surprise for Martha. She's been talking about you all day, Anna."

"Send Anna back home at about seven thirty, will you, Gladys?" Asked Joseph.

"I sure will. Come on in, Anna."

"Bye, Daddy. I love you."

"I love you, too, sweetie."

"Martha, look who's come to visit with you. It's Anna."

"Anna!" Martha shouted, as she ran to greet her.

"Look, Martha. Look what Santa left for you at my house!"

"Momma! Daddy! Look!" Martha screamed. "Santa didn't forget about me, after all. Look, he left these presents at Anna's. I told you he would come. I told you!"

Tears came to Rebecca's eyes. Frank looked down at the floor, then over to Reverend Twigg, bewildered. Reverend Twigg gave him a reassuring smile.

"Can I open them, Momma?"

"Oh, I don't know. I don't think you should open them until Christmas."

"Oh, Momma, *please?*"

"Well, Rebecca, under the circumstances, I don't see any harm that would come from letting Martha open just one of the gifts tonight, do you?" Reverend Twigg asked.

Martha's mother looked at her husband. "Frank?"

Afraid that if he spoke, he would not be able to control his emotions, Frank simply nodded his head, his eyes glazed over.

Martha picked out a gift to open from the stack before her. Her eyes stretched wide as she unwrapped the package. She peeled away the paper and opened the box within.

"Look, Momma! A new baby doll."

The only baby doll Martha ever had was one her mother fashioned from some old material she found. Martha took her new baby doll to show her mother.

"Why are you crying, Momma? Aren't you happy that I got this new baby doll?"

"I'm very happy, honey. I'm so happy that it just makes me cry," she said.

Rebecca held Martha tightly to her breast and sobbed. Martha's father couldn't take it any longer. He got up from his chair and went out onto the back porch. Reverend Twigg followed him to make sure he was alright. Putting his hand on Frank's shoulder, he said, "I know everything's going to turn out okay for you."

Frank wiped his eyes with his handkerchief, then he blew his nose and put his hankie into his back pocket. "I don't know, Ernest. I've been down on my luck for quite a while now."

"You must have faith, young man. I know that if you do, you will overcome all of this. I know you will."

"You all have been so very kind to us here. When our wagon broke down, I cursed God, Ernest. I was so mad, so frustrated, that I cursed God."

Frank paused a moment, and he started to choke up again. He tightened his lips and narrowed his eyes in an attempt to squint back his tears.

"I'm sure God will forgive you if you ask him to."

"Oh I have, Ernest, I have. You know, in many ways our wagon breaking down here in Myersdale was actually a blessing. I was so tired, and Rebecca and the kids were cold and hungry. I don't know how much further we could have gotten without a little help. Thanks, Ernest."

"God knows what's in our hearts and minds, Frank. He probably knew all of this. That may be why your wagon wheel broke here, you know? Why don't you stay on for a few days, at least through Christmas?"

"I appreciate the offer, but I have to get to Cumberland. There's a blacksmith there and I'm told he needs a helper. I have an old friend in Cumberland I think we can stay with until I get on my feet."

"Well, you're welcome to stay here."

"I know that, and I'm grateful, believe me."

Reverend Twigg put his arm around Frank's shoulder and said, "Let's go back inside. It's cold out here."

Anna and Martha were in the kitchen playing with Martha's new doll when Gladys came out to tell Anna that it was time for her to go home. How quickly the hour had passed. As Anna put on her coat, Martha asked her mother, "Can I go out and sit on the front porch for a minute with Anna to say good-bye?"

"Okay, but put on your coat and hat. I don't want you to catch cold."

Anna and Martha sat on the front porch, trying to squeeze out just a few more minutes together before they had to part. Anna pointed out to Martha the stars her father showed her. She remembered her wish, and just knew it would come true; part of it already had.

"You're a nice friend," Martha told Anna.

"You are, too."

"I wish we didn't have to leave in the morning. Reverend Twigg told Daddy we could stay for a few more days."

"Are you going to?" Anna asked, looking up with surprise.

"No. Daddy says we have to go. I'm going to miss you, Anna." Martha started to cry.

Anna hated to see anyone cry. She wanted to make her friend feel better.

"Don't cry. It'll be okay," Anna said in an attempt to console her. Her words of comfort had little effect.

"I'm scared," Martha said, and more tears rolled down her cheeks.

"Here. Take this," Anna said, pulling her ring from her finger and handing it Martha. "Mommy said it's worth money. Your daddy can sell it."

"But, Anna! I can't take your pretty ring. My daddy wouldn't allow it. Besides, it's your favorite thing, your lucky charm."

"My daddy says that if you have something that someone you like really needs, you should give it to that person. He says God loves a cheerful giver. You need food. And my ring will bring you good luck too," Anna said.

"Gee, Anna, I don't know."

"Here," Anna insisted, putting the ring in Martha's coat pocket. "But don't give it to your daddy until you're almost to Cumberland. Tell him it's a Christmas present from me to your family. He can buy food with the money he gets for it."

"Thank you, Anna. You're such a good friend."

The front door opened, causing the girls to jump. "Anna, it's half past seven, time for you to go home," Mrs. Twigg said as she poked her head out the door.

"Okay, Mrs. Twigg."

"Do you want me to walk you home?"

"No thanks, ma'am, I can walk by myself."

The two girls said good-bye, this time realizing they might never see each other again. Anna began walking home. As she walked, she thought about how Martha's Christmas might be brighter because of the gift of the ring. She was glad she could do something to help her friend. She could not help, however, feeling a bit of a loss, having given away her special ring. The longer she walked, the more reservations she had about whether or not she had done the right thing. The vision of her unsettling dream began playing in her head. She was startled by the sight of her long shadow following her in the night. The more she thought about the dream, the more frightened she became. She picked up her gait to a skip, then she broke into a full run, seeking the security of her home.

As she ran, the full weight of giving away her prized ring dawned on her. "What will Mommy and Daddy say? Will I be in trouble?" She wondered as she ran. She reached the house, breathless and almost in tears. Before entering, she stopped to compose herself.

"Did you have a nice visit with your friend?" her mother asked.

"Yeah, it was okay," she said flatly.

"Was Martha surprised about the gifts Santa left here for her?"

"Oh, yes. She was very surprised," Anna said in a somewhat distant voice.

She started up the stairs. "Where are you going?" her mother asked.

Without stopping, Anna replied, "I don't feel very good. I'm going to bed."

Hearing the bedroom door shut, Joseph and Elda looked at each other, puzzled by Anna's behavior.

"I wonder what's wrong with Anna," Elda said.

"I don't know," Joseph replied. "I'll go up and check on her."

Joseph opened the door and saw Anna sitting on the edge of her bed, tears streaming down her face. When she saw him she quickly tried to wipe away the tears.

"What's wrong, my dear?" he asked.

"Nothing, Daddy."

"You seem to be awfully upset for it to be nothing."

She began to whimper, and then burst into tears again. He sat down beside her, pulling her close to him, wondering what was wrong.

"What is it, Anna?"

"I've done something that will make you and Mommy mad at me."

"What, my child?"

"I gave away my ring to Martha."

"But why, Anna? Didn't you like your ring?"

"I loved my ring, Daddy, it was my favorite thing. That's why I feel so bad."

Anna began to cry loudly. Joseph hugged her tightly.

"Then why, my dear, if you loved your ring so much, did you give it away?"

"Today in Sunday school we learned about the joy of giving. And you said that if you have something that someone you like really needs, you should give it to them, even if it is something you like a whole lot. You said you shouldn't give grudgingly. You said God loves a cheerful giver. Martha's family is poor and they need help ... and ... and ..." Then Anna began crying again.

"Oh, so that's what all those questions were about on the way to the Twiggs' tonight."

"Yes," Anna said with a sniffle.

"Oh, Anna, what I said is true, but it doesn't mean you should just give your things away."

"But, I gave her my ring so her daddy can sell it to buy food. Are you mad at me, Daddy?"

Joseph had to think for a minute before he answered. "Well, Anna, Daddy had to work a lot of hours to buy you that ring. Mommy and Daddy bought it for you because that's all you talked about. I thought it meant more to you than that. So, yes, I'm a bit upset over this."

Her father's answer broke Anna's heart. She thought she had done a good thing, but now she wasn't sure.

"We'll talk about this more tomorrow. Get some sleep and you'll feel better." Before going back downstairs, Joseph bent over and kissed Anna on her forehead. "And, don't forget to say your prayers."

"I won't, Daddy."

The bedroom went dark when Joseph closed the door. Anna got up from her bed and walked to the window. Looking up at the stars, she began to pray.

"God, why is Daddy mad at me? I was just trying to help Martha and her family. I did what I thought You wanted me to do, and Daddy, too. I liked my ring, but Daddy said You don't want people to give things grudgingly, and that You like people who give to the needy. That's what Mrs. Olson said, too. Please make it so that Daddy's not mad. God bless Mommy and Daddy, Earl, Sis, Jule, Boopie, Dick, Tobi and Nelly. And, Please help Martha and her family. They need You. Amen."

❄ ❄ ❄

"What was the matter with Anna?" Elda asked as Joseph

walked into the living room.

"Oh, she's upset."

"About what? Did she and Martha get into an argument or something?

"No. She felt sorry for Martha and gave her ring to her."

"She gave her ring away?" Elda said with shock.

"Yes, she did."

"But why?"

"So Martha's father could sell it and use the money to buy food."

"What did you say to Anna?"

"Well … I think I might have been a little hard on her, especially since I may be partially responsible for this."

"What do you mean?"

"On the way over to the Twiggs' Anna was asking me all these questions."

"What kind of questions?"

"She wanted to know if a person had something they really liked, but someone they cared about needed it, should they give it to them."

"What did you tell her?"

"I told her yes. I told her what the Bible says about giving, and that's what she's been studying in Sunday school. I just never thought …" Joseph caught himself. It suddenly occurred to him what a wonderful thing Anna had done.

"Do you want to go over to the Twiggs' and talk to Martha's father about this?" Elda asked.

"No. No, that wouldn't be right. In fact, I'm a bit ashamed of myself for the way I reacted."

"What do you mean?"

"Well, here I am giving Anna a lecture about the good that comes from giving, and when she does what the scripture says, I condemn her. She has a good heart, Elda. We should be very proud of our daughter."

"It must have taken a lot of soul-searching for Anna to part with her ring."

"Yes. I'm sure it did. Elda, I feel terrible for the way I reacted. I was too hard on her. I should have praised her and told her that she made me proud."

"Well don't be too hard on yourself now, Joseph. You can tell her tomorrow," Elda said as she reached for his hand.

As Elda and Joseph walked up the stairs to turn in for the night, Joseph opened the door to Anna's room and walked to the side of her bed. He had hoped that she would still be awake so he could tell her he was sorry and that he was proud of her for her unselfishness. The dim light from the hall crept through the doorway and cast a soft glow on Anna's sleeping face. Joseph looked down at her angelic expression. She looked so innocent, with her arm around Teddy, holding him tightly. Joseph was moved. He knelt at the side of her bed. Placing his hand, gently, against her cheek, he prayed, thanking his Lord for the wonderful gifts God had given him and Elda - six beautiful children who made their house a home abounding with laughter, warmth, and humility, and overflowing with life and love.

Chapter X

It was the early morning of Christmas Eve. Joseph sat at the kitchen table drinking a cup of coffee, enjoying the last few minutes in the warmth of his home before going out into the cold December air to go to work. He was tired. He had difficulty sleeping the night before. He tossed and turned, preoccupied with thoughts of Anna. And, he was plagued with a new dream that reoccurred throughout the night.

He pondered the events of the previous evening. How he wished he could relive the moment when Anna told him she had given her ring to the little girl whose family was in need.

"Why was I so harsh?" he thought. "I'm supposed to be a Christian. Here, Anna does a Christian deed, and I tell her I'm upset with her." Joseph was ashamed of himself.

He desperately wanted to right things with Anna before he went off to work. Before going downstairs that morning, Joseph had stepped into Anna's bedroom hoping to talk to her, but as he tiptoed to the side of her bed, he saw that she was still asleep. He picked up Teddy, who had fallen to the floor, and placed him back in the bed beside her. Then, he bent over her and kissed her softly on the forehead before leaving the room.

As he took another sip of coffee, he began to think about the dream he had last night. This one was different. No angels, no Jesus, just the strange beautiful music that he heard in his previous dreams. The music was coming from a small shop across the street from where he stood. In his dream, he crossed the street, following the music into a dingy shop, but just as he opened the door, he would wake up. This happened time after time throughout the night.

He rose from his chair, paused for a second, then drained the last drop of coffee from his mug. He peeked out the kitchen window to see what the day was offering. It was still dark. The winter wind rattled the frost-covered glass in the windows.

Joseph glanced at the walnut cuckoo clock that hung on the dining room wall, anticipating the little wooden bird signaling the time for him to go. The clock sounded once, indicating it was half past five. Joseph pulled a gold pocket watch from his pocket to verify the hour. It looked small as it lay in the center of his hand.

He remembered when Elda had given him the watch as an anniversary gift, some six years ago. It meant so much to her. Without Joseph even knowing it, she had taken in laundry and made quilts to earn the money to buy it. Joseph was totally surprised when she gave it to him. The pocket watch was among his most precious belongings. Holding it in the palm of his hand, he could almost feel it ticking, just as he felt the beating of Elda's heart when he held her close. The watch face was beautiful, just like Elda's. It was fragile and delicate, just as she was. The watch was a symbol of their deep love and unyielding commitment to each other.

A gentle nudge on his shoulder interrupted his thoughts. Elda, arms outstretched, offered him his coat and hat.

"You'll be late," she said. Her generous smile made him want to stay. "Don't forget your lunch. I put something special in it for you."

Joseph leaned down and kissed Elda on the lips. "Good-bye, dear. I'll see you this evening when I return. I don't know what time it will be, but it shouldn't be too late. With a little luck, I'll make it back in time for the kids' pageant."

She looked up into his eyes. "I love you, Joseph. Be safe."

"I love you, too."

As he opened the door to leave, the frosty air bit into his face. The winter's dawn wind was stinging. As he walked, his feet disappeared in the fresh snow that had fallen during the night.

Up North Street he went, turning right onto Main. He stopped several times to look in the shop windows decorated for the holiday. He walked to the end of town to the train station. There, he would hitch a ride to work at the rail yard just outside of town.

When Joseph arrived, he rushed through the station to the freight train stopped on the tracks outside. He approached the dirty red caboose at the end of the train and was greeted by Stanley Taylor, the train's conductor.

Stan was a man of slight build. His pants always hung loosely on his hips. A turtleneck sweater formed a baggy ring of wool around his thin gullet. The thick lenses on his glasses made his eyes appear much larger than they actually were.

"Good morning, Joseph."

"Good morning, Stan. It's a cold one this morning," Joseph said as he grabbed the handrail and pulled himself aboard.

The train left the station and Joseph watched the tiny town

of Myersdale disappear into a horizon made gray by the approaching sunrise.

"Are your kids as excited about Christmas as mine are?" Stan asked.

"Yeah, they're pretty stirred up," replied Joseph.

"What's Santa going to drop off at the Beal house this year?"

Joseph felt a bit embarrassed by the question, because he really didn't know. Elda handled all of that.

"Oh, I'm not certain, but I'm sure he won't disappoint the children," Joseph said. "What's the news on the coal mine opening up on the mountain?" he asked, hoping to change the subject.

"I hear it's a go. If it is, I guess we'll be pretty busy."

The train whistled loudly, an indication that it was approaching the next stop. This served well as a transition point in the conversation. Stan began to prepare for the stop, and Joseph rose to look out the window as they approached the rail yard. The sun was beginning to creep up over the horizon, painting the sky red and casting shadows from the snowdrifts that lay on the ground like miniature mountains.

The train jerked suddenly, knocking Joseph off balance; he fell back into his seat with a thud. Stan looked down at Joseph with momentary concern, and then they both began to laugh. The train stopped and Joseph rose to his feet again to exit.

"Have a good day, now," Stan said, still laughing as Joseph passed him heading for the door of the caboose.

"You do the same, Stan," Joseph said, shaking his head as he opened the door to leave.

Joseph walked down the tracks to the machine shop, where

he grabbed a cup of brew before continuing down the tracks to his train. Nearing the locomotive, he heard it huffing and puffing as it spit steam and billowed smoke from its stack. It seemed to be impatiently waiting to begin its journey. Joseph stopped, momentarily, to admire the power of the machine before he climbed aboard.

When he entered the cab of the locomotive Joseph received a robust greeting from his friend, Christopher Mathers, the fireman on the locomotive. It was his job to tend the fire in the boiler that provided the vessel's power. The job demanded much strength and endurance, as he was required to shovel countless loads of coal into the fire on each run to keep the engine going. Christopher was a large fellow with ample strength for the task, a jolly Scotsman who was a bit rough around the edges.

"Merry Christmas to ya, Joseph!" Christopher roared.

"Morning, Christopher," said Joseph to his friend. "Do you have this thing ready to go?"

"She's a-ready, Joseph."

"Is everyone aboard?"

"Yeah. They're all back there a-waitin' ta go."

The remainder of the crew was stationed in the caboose, a bit more hospitable place to be on such a chilly morning. Lee McCleskey was the train's conductor. With him in the caboose were Tom Smith and John Hill, the two brakemen assigned to the train.

While Joseph readied the engine for departure, he reached into his coat pocket to retrieve a pouch of chewing tobacco. He opened the pouch, dipped his hand deep inside, pulled out a sizable wad, and stuffed it into his mouth, causing his cheek to bulge. Mail Pouch was his brand. Joseph had few vices in life, but this was one.

Today, they would haul a trainload of coal to Brunswick, Maryland, and bring back another train to Myersdale. It would be an easy run, Joseph thought. Just down and back. They should be back before supper.

Joseph pulled his watch from his pocket and checked the time. He hesitated as he saw his reflection in the face of his watch. He couldn't help thinking about Anna. He truly regretted his reaction to her giving away her ring. Again he wondered about the dreams he had been having, and what they meant.

"Watch broke, Joseph?" Christopher asked, curious to know why Joseph's attention was fixed on the gold timepiece he held in his hand.

"No," Joseph said in a low tone. "I was just thinking."

Joseph got the signal to depart. He sounded the train's whistle to alert the crew they were about to leave. He eased the throttle forward and the steam-driven piston began to move. The powerful locomotive began to grind down the tracks leading away from the station. It set out slowly, laboring under the weight of hundreds of tons of western Pennsylvania coal. As the cars began to move, they jolted and banged as the couplers between them became taut. When the locomotive gained speed, Joseph could feel the power he controlled. He loved that feeling.

While the train headed down the tracks, Christopher shoveled coal into the firebox. It was important that the fireman and engineer work closely together to get maximum efficiency and force from the mighty steam-powered engine.

After the fire was blazing sufficiently to build up the needed steam, Christopher took a breather. He sat across the cab from Joseph and looked over the gauges. When he finished, he engaged Joseph in some conversation about the holiday. The noise of the steam engine was loud, making it difficult to hear. They had to shout in order to hear each other when they spoke.

"I got little Jimmy a red wagon fer Santa to put under the tree," boasted Christopher proudly, in his best Scottish accent. "And Belinda will be surprised when she sees the new coat and hat I bought fer her," he continued. "How about you, Joseph? What have ya gotten fer Elda and the kids?"

"Well, I … the pressure's going down! Better bring the temperature up," Joseph shouted, dispatching Christopher to tend the fire, thus breaking off the conversation that made him feel so ill at ease.

The train rolled down the mountain. The sun, which by now had moved over the horizon, illuminated the day. Joseph looked out the window of the engine at the passing winter landscape. His thoughts returned to Anna, to the enigmatic dreams, and the events of the past several days.

"They're sayin' there's a winter storm a-comin' in over the mountains, Joseph," barked Christopher from the back of the locomotive.

Joseph, in deep thought, said nothing. He didn't even hear his friend.

"Joseph? Joseph!" Christopher shouted. "Are you awake up there, fer cryin' out loud?"

Joseph's head jerked to attention, almost as if he had dozed off momentarily. His senses renewed, he resumed the duties associated with piloting the train. But the nagging feelings he had about Anna and his curiosity about the mysterious visions would resurface several more times during the trip.

The scenery on this run was magnificent. The train snaked its way through the mountains and along the river, offering a splendid spectacle.

When the train approached a sharp curve, Joseph reached overhead and pulled the cord on the train's whistle, letting out a shrill scream that accompanied the speeding locomotive down the canyon. The train leaned hard to the right as it struggled to stay on the tracks.

Joseph noticed that the bright sun was beginning to give way to some ominous dark clouds that were hovering over the mountains. He yelled back to Christopher, "Looks like we're in for a storm."

Christopher looked back at Joseph without saying a word. He was bewildered by Joseph's strange manner. "I know. That's what I was tellin' ya a-ways back!" Christopher shouted, somewhat annoyed.

The train was approaching the Brunswick yard. Joseph began to reduce speed and prepare for their arrival. With a few short blasts on the whistle, he signaled the brakemen, who were riding in the caboose, to apply the brakes. Slowly the train came to rest on the tracks in the Brunswick yard. The crew exited the train, leaving it hyperventilating on the tracks, awaiting the fresh crew that would take it on to Baltimore.

Chapter XI

The morning passed quickly for Elda. There were too many things to do and too little time to do them. There was the turkey to buy, the stuffing to prepare, the cranberry sauce to fix, and the pies to bake - pumpkin, cherry, and apple. It seemed the Beals could never get their fill of Elda's pies.

Sis and Jule were helping by baking some cookies. Boopie stood nearby, undoubtedly waiting for an opening to inflict mischief on his sisters. He soon found it.

"Stop it, Boopie!"

"What, Sis? I didn't do anything!" But the evidence of his misdeed was apparent on his face, as crumbs and chocolate covered his lips, and his cheeks protruded from the volume of cookies he had swiftly crammed into his mouth.

"I saw you sneak those cookies," said Sis. "Now get out of here before you eat them all."

She playfully chased him around the table with a rolling pin. Elda looked over and laughed, shaking her head.

Anna seemed out of sorts. She picked at her breakfast, hardly eating a thing. Then, she rescued Tobi from the torment of Boopie and Dick and retreated to her room. She lay on her bed, finding solace in the raspy rattle of her cat's purr. Tobi was sprawled out on her chest, his front paws kneading her wool sweater. As she stroked his soft fur, her thoughts returned to last

113

night. She felt empty.

"I miss my ring," she told Tobi. "I thought Daddy would be proud of me, but instead, I made him mad."

The thought of her father being angry with her was very upsetting. She always did everything she could to please him. Her eyes moistened as she thought about what she had done. She was still confused. In Sunday school, she had learned the lesson of giving.

"Mrs. Olson said that it was good to give, especially to the poor," Anna continued her one-way conversation with her cat.

"Martha and her family certainly are poor," she thought. "Daddy said if you have something you really like a lot, and someone you care about needs it, you should give it to them. He said God loves a cheerful giver. Mommy and Daddy were so proud of me when I gave Martha my gloves." She reasoned that the ring helped Martha and her family much more than the gloves, so they should be even more proud of her.

She thought about the passage from proverbs she recited in Sunday school. Then she said it aloud: "He that giveth unto the poor shall not lack, but he who hideth his eyes shall have many a curse."

"Many a curse," she thought. "How terrible that would be."

She recalled the dream that she had a few nights before about Jesus. Even now, when she closed her eyes, she still had a vivid image of Jesus holding out his hand to her, asking her to give him her ring. She drifted back into the dream and the image became more clear. Frightened, she quickly opened her eyes and gave Tobi a slight squeeze. His purr was becoming louder, and he nudged his head up under her chin, as if asking her to continue stroking his back.

"Okay, okay," she said, and she resumed petting him.

Her thoughts drifted to Martha. She wondered how her journey to Cumberland was going. She hoped the gloves she gave her would keep her hands warm. Where would they spend Christmas Eve? It was a good thing Santa dropped Martha's gifts off at her house. He probably wouldn't be able to find her otherwise, she reasoned. She wondered if she would she ever see her friend again.

Anna continued to wrestle with the issue of the ring. Should she have given it to Martha or not? Finally she was comfortable with her decision. She knew, in her heart, that she had done a good thing.

"I'm glad I gave my ring to Martha," she told Tobi in a confident voice.

The bedroom door burst open. Tobi, fearing it was one of the boys, sought refuge under Anna's bed. Her sisters' laughter preceded them into the room, arousing Anna.

"What's wrong, Anna?" Jule asked with concern, as the door swung open. "Don't you feel good?"

"I feel okay."

"Well, what's wrong then? Did you forget to tell Santa about something you want?"

"Naaaa. I was just talking to Tobi."

"Come on downstairs. We're about to put the frosting on the cookies."

"Yeah," Sis said, "And you can lick the bowl when we're finished."

Anna dashed down the stairs with her sisters and raced into

the kitchen. They sat at the table, scooping gobs of white icing out of a blue glass bowl, then spreading it generously on the cookies they had made. Elda, sensing that Anna was not quite herself, walked up behind her. She wrapped her arms around Anna and gave her a big hug and a kiss on the cheek.

"Hey there, love bug!" Elda said, in an effort to cheer her up. "I'll bet Santa has a bag full of surprises for you. You've been such a good little girl this year."

Anna smiled and looked up over her shoulder at her mother.

"Here, Mommy, this one's for you," she said offering her mother the cookie she was glazing. Elda took a bite of the cookie and a smile emerged on her face. Having her children so near gave her a warm feeling.

❋ ❋ ❋

The sky over Brunswick was gloomy, a sharp contrast to the mood in the streets. Everywhere, townsfolk hustled about merrily, doing their last-minute shopping. The town was abuzz with people filled with the spirit of Christmas. Joseph found the cheerful mood to be contagious.

He had some time to kill while he and his crew waited for his train to arrive and be readied for the return trip to Myersdale. Strolling along the streets of Brunswick, Joseph looked at all the beautiful decorations. Normally, he would not have noticed such things, but for some reason, he felt different about the decorations this Christmas season. This year, he saw many things that he failed to recognize in the past. He watched the sparkle in the children's eyes as they tugged on their mothers' arms, pulling them to the line where Santa was listening to their Christmas wishes.

Joseph walked by one shop where a window display caught his attention. It was a Nativity scene beneath a Christmas tree. Toys surrounded the tree: tin soldiers, dolls, a wagon, and many other things that would thrill little boys and girls. He imagined the look on his own children's faces as they open their presents on Christmas morning. As a child, he never had the joyful experience of opening gifts on Christmas, nor the delight of a brightly decorated tree.

The bells of the town's church struck eleven times. By habit, Joseph pulled out his pocket watch to see if it matched the clock. He was hungry, so he sat down on a bench and opened his lunch pail. He proceeded to eat its contents: two egg sandwiches, an apple and, of course, a large piece of Elda's delicious banana bread. After he finished, he glanced down, and at the bottom of his lunch pail he noticed a hankie rolled up with a red ribbon tied around it. Curious, he untied the ribbon, unrolled the hankie and discovered a note inside.

December 24, 1918

My Dearest Darling,

I just wanted to tell you how much you mean to me. Your strength and wisdom have served all of us well. Your warm smile and gentle manner add a tender quality to your strong resolve. My heart burns with love for you, the intensity of which grows each day. I want to assure you, I respect your feelings toward Christmas.

The children and I share your deep faith and appreciation for the true meaning of the holiday. Thank you for teaching the children that meaning. What Anna did yesterday shows that she truly understands.

Thank you for your patience in allowing me and the children to enjoy the lighter side of Christmas, as well as the spiritual side. I look forward to your home-coming tonight and to enjoying this Holy Eve together as a loving family. We'll be waiting for you.

Merry Christmas, Joseph.

All my love,

Elda

P.S. I hope you liked the banana bread.

The note brought a smile to Joseph's face, as he placed it back in his lunch pail. Still holding the handkerchief that contained the letter, he smelled the fragrance of Elda's favorite perfume. He raised the perfume-soaked linen to his nose and inhaled deeply. He could see Elda's image as he closed his eyes and relished her scent.

The sky darkened and snow began to fall. Joseph got up from the bench and continued to make his way through the streets of the town. He passed a group of carolers singing "Silent Night", and he stopped to listen to their soothing hymn.

While he stood listening, his attention was drawn to a small shop across the street. Oddly, it was the only shop not decorated for the holiday. Something about it seemed peculiar. Then he realized it was the shop he had seen in his dream the night before, the shop from which the music came. Joseph had an uncomfortable feeling in the pit of his stomach but his curiosity lured him toward the tiny shop. With great apprehension, he crossed the street, not knowing what to expect. As he opened the front door, a small bell which hung over the entrance announced his arrival. Inside, the shop was dirty and had a strong musky odor. Most of the shelves were practically empty. A disheveled woman worked behind the counter. She didn't speak to him when he entered.

He browsed through the drab little shop, meandering from aisle to aisle. Most of the shelves had been picked over. The items that remained appeared to be the remnants of someone's life: a silver hairbrush and mirror, a used silver tea server, a rack of children's dresses and books.

High on a dust-covered shelf, Joseph noticed a beautiful jewelry box. Standing on a stool, he retrieved it. He blew the dust from its top revealing a brass plate with the inscription "Sarah". Upon opening it, he discovered that the box was empty. Joseph wound the key that protruded from its side and a lovely melody began to play. The song brightened the otherwise somber ambience of the room. It also gave cause for the woman behind the counter to look up at him for the first time. Joseph listened and the familiarity of the tune became obvious - it was the melody that had accompanied his dreams. Startled, he quickly slammed the lid; the experience sent chills up his back.

He eased the box back onto the shelf and slowly walked up the aisle. The woman behind the counter looked frail and vulnerable, her hair was unkempt. The troubled expression on her face was haunting. She seemed heavily burdened and sad. Joseph scanned the objects under the smudged glass counter and his eyes came to rest upon a small golden ring.

"May I see that ring, please?"

Joseph got no reply or recognition. He spoke again, a little louder.

"Excuse me, ma'am. May I please see that ring you have behind the counter?"

Without saying a word, she retrieved the ring and handed it to him. Joseph held the ring in his hand and realized his heart was pounding in his chest. A strange sensation came over him, the same sensation he experienced while holding the ring in his dream. He could not believe his eyes. This was identical to the ring he had seen in his night visions, unmistakably, right down to the small ruby setting in the ring's elaborately carved face.

His mind flashed back to the image of Jesus and what he had said, telling him to take the ring, that it would bring others great joy.

"What did he mean?" Joseph thought. He pondered the

similarity to Anna's dream. He was confused, even a bit frightened, by the mystery of what was unfolding.

"Is this ring for sale?" he asked, his voice quivering.

"I'm afraid it is," replied the woman without even looking up.

"Anna should have this ring," he thought.

"How much is it?" He said.

He got no answer.

"How much for the ring?" he repeated louder, almost in a panic.

The woman appeared visibly shaken, as thought she really did not want him to buy it.

"Why was she selling it then, if she didn't want anyone to buy it?" he thought.

"Six dollars and fifty cents," she answered sharply.

"That's a lot," Joseph thought. More than he had. But he knew he must get this ring for Anna. She deserved it as a reward for her unselfish act.

"All I have is five dollars and twenty cents. Will you let me have it for that?"

The woman thought for a moment, and then reluctantly said, "Alright. Five dollars and twenty cents, and not a penny less."

"I'll take it!"

As Joseph reached into his pocket for his money, he noticed the portrait of a young girl hanging on the wall behind the woman. He observed that the girl was about Anna's age, and she was wearing the ring that he now held in his hand. When he handed the woman his money, he saw that she was quietly weeping.

"Excuse me, ma'am, but why are you crying? Have I done something to upset you?"

She didn't answer him.

"What is it?" he asked again.

"It's ... it's nothing, sir. It's just ..." Then she broke down and began to cry openly. Joseph reached out and held her hands in an effort to soothe her. She composed herself and said, "The girl in that portrait is my daughter, Sarah. Last year, my husband and Sarah were killed in a tragic accident. She was my only child." The woman began to weep again.

"I'm so sorry," Joseph said.

"The bank is foreclosing on the shop and the house is next, so I'm forced to sell everything, even my personal things. Even ... even ... Sarah's ring." The woman broke down again. "It's all I have left of her."

Joseph felt terrible. "I had no idea."

"How could you?"

"I can't take this ring. You should keep it."

"No, I have to sell it. I need the money," she said.

"But I can't take it, not under these circumstances."

"Nonsense! I have to sell it, if not to you, then to someone else. You wanted the ring, now take it, please."

"I'm sorry, but I just can't."

"Who where you buying it for, anyway?"

"My daughter, Anna."

"How old is Anna?"

"Nine."

"My Sarah was nine when she left me."

"She was a beautiful young girl," Joseph said as he looked up at her portrait.

"Were you buying the ring for Anna as a Christmas gift?"

"Well, not exactly."

"What do you mean?"

Joseph told the woman the touching story about what Anna had done the previous day. After hearing the tale, the woman smiled and said, "Your Anna has made me smile for the first time since I lost my beloved Sarah. You're a lucky man to have such a special little girl. Take the ring, and give it to Anna as a gift from me. I won't take a dime of your money for it."

"But …"

"Don't argue," she said with a sad smile.

"But I can't take the ring and not pay you for it. Besides, you need the money."

"The ring is not about money. It's about love. I want your Anna to have this ring. Now take it and be gone!"

The woman began to weep again, but said, "These are tears of joy, not sadness. I'm truly happy that Sarah's ring is going to a little girl like Anna."

"Here, take my money, please. I beg you."

"Thank you, but I don't want your money. I want to give this ring to Anna. I insist!"

"Alright then," Joseph conceded. "But I want to pay you for that jewelry box that plays the sweet music, and I won't take no for an answer. How much is it?"

"One dollar and seventy-five cents," she answered.

"How about two dollars and fifty cents," Joseph countered with a grin.

"That's too much."

"Two dollars and fifty-five cents?" Joseph said, raising his bid. "And not a penny less!"

"We have a deal, but you sure drive a hard bargain," the woman said in jest. Then she put out her right hand for Joseph to close the deal.

As she took the money, the woman looked at Joseph very seriously and said, "Thank you for coming into my shop today. And thank you for telling me about your daughter, Anna. The two of you certainly brightened my spirits. Merry Christmas, sir."

"The name's Joseph."

"Mine's Madeline. Merry Christmas, Joseph."

"Merry Christmas, Madeline," Joseph replied with a departing smile.

Joseph crossed the narrow avenue in front of the shop and came upon the Christmas carolers he had passed earlier. He paused, listening to their last refrain of "O' Holy Night". When they had finished, he called out to the ensemble's leader.

"Excuse me, sir? Can you help me?"

"Help you?" the man replied. "With what?"

Pointing to the shop he'd just left, Joseph said, "There's a lonely woman in the shop across the street. She is very sad and in need of some cheer."

"What's that?" the man asked, not fully understanding what Joseph wanted him to do.

"Here," Joseph said, emptying the remaining money from his pocket into the jewelry box he purchased from the woman. "Take this money and this box to the lady in that shop and sing to her like you've never sung before. This is a time of great despair for her and she could use your help and encouragement."

"What's the matter with her?" asked one of the carolers.

Joseph told them her story.

"That's terrible," said the group's leader. Taking the jewelry box from Joseph, the man said to his friends, "Let's pass this box among us and add to the sum this gentleman has offered."

"Pass it over here," yelled one of the singers in the group.

"Here's fifty cents," said another.

The carolers gave generously as the box made its rounds. Even some passersby were moved to contribute. When the box was returned to the leader of the group, it was overflowing with money.

"This ought to help that poor lady out," said the man to Joseph. "Now let's go see if we can't cheer her spirits with song," he said as he led the group across the street, singing "O' Little Town of Bethlehem".

"Thank you all for your kindness," Joseph called out to them. "Her name is Madeline. When you give her the box, please tell her that Anna said 'Merry Christmas!'"

Joseph watched from across the street as the carolers entered the shop. As he stood there, he could hear their inspiring songs. He took the golden ring from his pocket. Cradling it in the palm of his hand, he stared at it, wondering what it was all about. The dreams and the music all seemed so strange, yet, mysteriously, it all fit together. Anna's generosity had come full circle and now she would receive her proper reward.

"There must be something very special, very powerful about

this ring," he thought.

His dreams - and Anna's - foretold all of this. Now, there was absolutely no doubt in Joseph's mind that he was wrong about scolding Anna for giving her ring to Martha. He couldn't wait to get home to set things right with her. He wanted to tell her he was sorry for doubting the goodness of her deed.

"I'll slip the ring on Anna's finger while she sleeps," he thought. "That way she won't know where it came from. Someday, when she grows up, I'll tell her the story behind this incredible ring."

Joseph looked up to the sky and thanked God for the blessing he had just received. While he prayed, snowflakes hit his face and quickly melted. A winter storm was rapidly descending; the snow fell more briskly, covering the streets of the town. The wind began to whip and whirl. Joseph looked down to measure the snow's accumulation against his boots. It was higher than his ankles. He reached into his coat and fetched his chewing tobacco. He took one last glance across the street at the woman's shop as he inserted a pinch of tobacco into his mouth, stuffing it tightly against the inside of his cheek. Then, he turned and began his hike back to the station. As he disappeared around the corner at the end of the street, he could still hear the faint harmonies of the carolers.

Chapter XII

*M*iles away, back in Myersdale, there was much chatter and lively laughter coming from Joseph's home. The children were overcome with excitement as they helped their mother ready the house for the festivities of the coming evening and following day.

Earlier in the afternoon, Elda had taken the children to Town Square where Santa made a brief appearance. He gave each of the kids a piece of maple candy, Boopie got three pieces. They shopped for the Christmas turkey, made candy and cookies, hung their stockings along the wooden staircase and fashioned a Yule log from pine, trimmed with sweet-scented balsam branches. It looked rather smart as the centerpiece on the dining room table. Throughout the day, snow flurries fell intermittently from the mixture of clouds and blue sky.

"Pass me some more popped corn," Jule requested.

Anna brought the bowl to her older sister, who was stringing popcorn on thread as garland for the tree. Sis was busily doing the same with cranberries. Dick and Boopie were acting foolish, and singing Christmas carols off key.

"You better hurry up, Sis," Boopie teased. "Santa is coming tonight, you know. He'll be needing that garland to decorate the tree."

Sis sent a cranberry sailing over his head.

"Missed me, missed me, ha, ha!"

This brought a laugh from the rest of the children.

"Have you practiced your lines, Anna?" Elda asked.

"Not yet, Mommy, but I will."

"It will be seven o'clock before you know it."

"Okay, Mommy, I'll practice in a minute."

On the way to her room to fetch her script, Anna was drawn to the Nativity scene. Staring at the wooden stable, she blocked out all the noise in the house. She noticed how proud and happy Mary seemed as she looked down at her newborn child. The Christ child looked so little and cute. It was hard for Anna to imagine that little baby as her Savior. He was so small and so delicate, so dependent upon Mary. Anna couldn't resist the urge to pick up the figure of baby Jesus and hold it in her hand. She held it for a moment before returning it to its proper place in the manger.

As Anna withdrew her hand from the Nativity, she noticed a slight red circle around the finger where her favorite ring had fit tightly against her skin. It was a fading reminder of the cherished gift she had received from her parents. She missed her ring, but she knew that long after the red circle on her finger faded, she would remember how happy she had made Martha and her family. The feeling that filled Anna's her heart after helping that poor family was, to her, a sacred gift from Jesus, who taught her how to give.

❄ ❄ ❄

By the time Joseph got back to the station, he was covered with snow. The storm was in full fury. When he walked into the lobby, his friend, Christopher hailed him.

"I'm afraid I've got a bit of bad news fer ya, Joseph."

"Bad news?"

"Our train's been delayed. All the tracks leadin' inta Brunswick are blocked by driftin' snow. Our train may not make it through 'til the bloody storm clears. That may not be 'til tomorrow." Then he hesitated, "I don't want to miss Christmas with ma family, Joseph."

Joseph's heart sank. "Not this Christmas," he thought. He wanted so badly to get home to Anna.

"Well, let's wait and see what happens before we surrender," he said optimistically.

"They got a card game goin' in the storeroom ta pass the time. Do ya wanna get in a game?"

"No. You go ahead, Christopher. I've got some thinking to do. I may join you later."

Joseph accompanied Christopher back to the storeroom where he got a cup of hot coffee. He then found a quiet corner in the lobby by the window where he could look out over the river. The storm was raging. The wind was blowing the snow with such force that, at times, all Joseph could see was nothing but a wall of white.

Looking up at the ceiling, Joseph whispered, "Dear Lord, please help me get back home tonight. I made a terrible mistake last night with Anna. I need to straighten it out. I want her to feel good about what she has done. I want to tell her how proud I am of her for making that family's Christmas so special. I want her to understand how special this Christmas is because of her. Please, dear God, I beg this of You."

Joseph kept trying to make sense of the last few days. Were the visions he and Anna saw merely dreams? Or was Jesus actually guiding them to do his work? Did He lead Anna to that little girl whose family was penniless and down on its luck? Was her dream a vision from Jesus telling her that she would be giving her ring and her heart to Him by helping the little girl's family? Was He leading Joseph to that pitiful woman in the dirty little shop in Brunswick? Joseph had more questions than he had answers. He couldn't understand it all. Nor could he explain it. But he had total faith and trust in his God.

"Sometimes a little faith is better than a lot of understanding," he thought.

Joseph walked over to George Brice's office to check the status of the incoming trains. George was the station agent in charge of the Brunswick station.

"Any news?" Joseph asked.

George shook his head. "The tracks are still closed. The snow fighters are working as hard as they can, but every time they get the tracks cleared, the snow drifts back across. They say it's almost useless to keep trying."

Joseph peered out the window. "It doesn't look like it's letting up either. Dang, George! I've just got to get home for Christmas. I've got to!"

"I'm sorry. They're doing all they can. I'll let you know as soon I hear something."

Joseph banged his fist hard into his hand and walked away. All of the waiting was making him edgy. As it became more apparent he would be spending Christmas there in Brunswick, his anger mounted. Joseph was generally an even-tempered sort. It was a rare occasion when he displayed any anger. The last time that happened was a few years ago. Joseph had been walking back to the Brunswick station when he came upon a group of railroaders harassing an old drunkard in front of the tavern down the street. Joseph stood up for the helpless old man, even physically challenging the bunch if they didn't let the poor man alone.

Joseph walked back to the supply room to talk to Christopher.

"Joseph. Would ya like to sit in on a hand?" his friend asked.

"No, Christopher. I don't really feel like playing cards right now. If they don't get the tracks clear, we'll have the whole night to play, tomorrow too!"

"What's the word, Joseph?" asked Lee, who sat across from Christopher at the table.

"It doesn't look good for us getting out of here tonight, unless there's a miracle."

"What did George say?" Christopher asked.

"He said the tracks keep drifting closed. They're thinking about giving up until the storm is over."

"I'm foldin', guys," Christopher said, tossing his cards onto the flimsy table. He too was troubled at the prospect of being stranded away from his family for Christmas. He walked over to the coffeepot and poured two cups of coffee, handing one to Joseph. Together, they walked out to the lobby, which was empty and very quiet. Their voices echoed off the towering ceiling. It was late afternoon by now, and it had been snowing for hours.

"Do you want ta go to the hotel and get a room, Joseph?"

"No. I'm not ready to give up hope yet. Besides, I have no money."

They sat quietly for several minutes. Then, Joseph broke the silence.

"It's important that I get home tonight, Christopher. I have something very important to do, and it must be done tonight."

Joseph pulled the golden ring from his pocket and showed it to his friend.

"That's an exquisite ring, Joseph. One more beautiful I've yet ta see. Who's it for?"

"It's for Anna. This is an extraordinary ring. It is blessed."

"What d' ya mean?"

"Christopher, do you believe in God?"

"Well, of course I do, Joseph! What kind of question is that?"

"I mean … do you really believe?"

"Yes. Yes! I really do believe in God. Maybe not as strongly as you, Joseph, but surely I do believe. What does all this have ta do with the ring, anyway?"

"A few days ago, I started having strange dreams."

"What kind of dreams?"

"Well, I was dreaming about Jesus. He would appear, hold out a ring, and ask me to take it. He said the ring would bring others great joy. And music accompanied these dreams."

"Music? What kinda music?"

"I don't know, it was a sweet song that I never heard before."

"Alright, Joseph. But what does all this have ta do with the ring?"

Holding out the ring, Joseph said, "This is the ring Christopher! This is the ring that I saw in my dreams."

"You're jokin' with me, eh, Joseph?"

"Do I look like I'm joking?" Joseph snapped.

"Where did ya get the ring?"

"I got it in a shop here in Brunswick."

He went on to tell Christopher about how he was led to the shop by the sound of the music and by the vision of the shop from his dreams. He recounted his conversation with the woman, and how she was moved to give him her daughter's ring. He told him about Anna's dream and about how she gave her ring to Martha. After he finished, he stood up, clenched his fists at his sides, and said, "You probably think I'm a darn fool!" He walked away shaking his head, embarrassed and frustration that he had been so open about his experience.

"Joseph. Joseph!" Christopher shouted as he followed him down the hall. "Joseph," he said, grabbing him by the shoulder and turning him around. "I don't think you're a fool! Not fer this. I believe ya, and I want ta help. You're ma friend, Joseph. Why wouldn't I want ta help ma friend?"

"I'm sorry I doubted you. I was out of line. I'm just running out of patience sitting around here, waiting."

"Ya must have faith, ma friend. If what you're sayin' is true, have faith. You'll get ta see Anna tonight."

Time was running out. The sky darkened as early evening approached. The storm had subsided somewhat; the wind was silent, at least for now.

"Joseph, I've got some good news!" George yelled across the

lobby from the dispatcher's booth. "Your train broke through the drifts and it's on its way. It should be here in thirty minutes, if all goes well."

Joseph's prayer was answered. He grabbed Christopher and gave him a big bear hug. Christopher let out a blaring howl, "Yahoo! We're goin' home!"

"Let's go get the guys!" Joseph said to his friend.

❄ ❄ ❄

Time passed and Joseph paced impatiently. It had now been forty-two minutes since George made the announcement, but the train still hadn't arrived. Joseph's anxiety was at its peak. His jaw was clenched tightly, his teeth grinding.

"Here it comes down the tracks, Joseph. I can see it!" Christopher shouted. He was every bit as excited as Joseph to be going home. Lee, Tom, and John were slapping each other's backs.

The train limped into the station. The crew disembarked and entered the terminal. The engineer looked weary.

"It's a bad night out there," he told Joseph. "I don't think this train is going any further tonight."

George called Joseph over to the dispatcher's booth. "Track conditions to the west aren't good, Joseph. I think we should call it a night rather than risk you being stranded along the tracks between here and Myersdale," George concluded. "Why don't you go down to the hotel and get a room for the night?"

"No, George, I can't! Try to understand I have to get home tonight. It's important. I know we can make it."

"My recommendation is that you not leave the station tonight. But I'll leave the final decision up to you and your crew. Why don't you see what the others have to say?"

Joseph met with his crew and, to the man, they agreed that they wanted to take the risk of running the train through the snowbound mountains to Myersdale. They all had wives and children there, except for John Hill, who was a bit on the wild side and unattached.

Joseph went back to George and advised him of the crew's decision. Though George had the power to overrule, he didn't. Joseph and his crew left the station to board the locomotive.

Chapter XIII

As the train pulled away from the Brunswick station, Joseph looked ahead into the darkness. The light from the engine shone dimly on the snow-covered tracks. The wind began to pick up again, tossing the snow in every direction before it could reach the ground.

Joseph dug deep into the pouch he carried in his coat pocket for another wad of chew. It would ease the tightness in his jaw. Tension on the train was high; each man wondered if he had made a wise decision.

The train sped along, plowing the snow high into the air, making it difficult for Joseph to see. He cautiously backed off the throttle, driving blindly through a thick sheet of white.

Christopher hastily shoveled coal into the inferno that powered the train. It was a strenuous task, one made even more arduous by the long day of waiting and wondering. Joseph opened the window of the engine and stuck his head outside to look west, up the tracks. The freezing air stung his face. He squinted to see through the blowing snow but visibility was poor - he could not see very far ahead. Trusting his intuition, he pushed the throttle forward. The locomotive strained as it trekked through the snow. Christopher worked tirelessly, like a machine, methodically throwing black nuggets of coal into the blazing firebox by the shovel full.

As they proceeded into the night, the weather worsened. The crew was on its own now; there were no snow fighters clearing the tracks ahead of them.

The Myersdale-bound freight powered on uneventfully for about two hours, but Joseph was well aware that the worst lay ahead. They were approaching the mountains, where they would face their final and most difficult obstacle.

Christopher continued to labor feverishly to feed the hungry fire. Joseph opened the throttle in an effort to get a run for the mountains ahead. The train picked up speed but so did the snow and wind, icing over the front of the locomotive.

Up the mountain they sped, pushing the iron horse to its limit, and beyond. When they cleared the first summit, Joseph breathed a sigh of relief, when suddenly the train began to lose momentum. Joseph inched the throttle forward, but the engine did not respond. Sluggishly, it labored up the tracks. Joseph opened the window and looked outside. Drifted snow lay heavy across the tracks before them. Their velocity diminished to a crawl until, finally, the train came to a discouraging halt.

The worst had finally happened. They were stuck in a snow-drift. Joseph hung his head and shook it in resignation. Christopher, frustrated and exhausted, angrily threw his shovel back into the coal car.

"No!" yelled Joseph as loud as he could. He banged his clenched fist onto the windowsill.

Christopher expressed his disappointment more colorfully, with a string of profanities made almost indistinguishable by his heavy Scottish brogue.

❄ ❄ ❄

"Hurry up, children. We'll be late!" prodded Elda, as she gathered them up and shepherded them out the front door.

"Do you have your hymn books?" she asked Sis and Jule.

"Anna, don't forget your scarf."

There was the usual uproar whenever trying to move the entire tribe along in the same direction, especially if they were on a timetable.

They walked up the street to the church and a heavy snow began to fall.

"Boopie, slow down and wait for the rest of us!" Elda said, as she dragged Dick along against his will.

"Mommy, I don't want to be a wise guy," young Dick protested, looking up at her.

"That's wise *man*," she corrected him.

"I don't want to be one of them either."

"You'll do fine," she reassured him.

"Do you think Daddy's going to make it home in time?" Anna asked.

"He may." Elda tried to project optimism in her voice, but inside, she was doubtful.

"I hope he does," said Sis. "I want him to hear me sing my song."

Ironically, the church seemed more like pandemonium. The atmosphere inside could best be described as controlled disorder. There was a backlog at the front door as people crowded to get in out of the snow. Children dressed as shepherds, wise men, sheep, and cows pushed through the aisles, deserting parents in search of Sunday school teachers who were attempting to bring order to the place. The state of excitement and anxiety was high, exceeded only by the state of confusion.

The pageant organizers soon gained control of the cast. The organ began to play a hymn and miraculously, the chaos gave way to order. A hush came over the audience in anticipation of the program's beginning.

Elda felt a tap on her shoulder. She turned to discover Belinda Mathers, Christopher's wife, sitting behind her.

"Did you hear?" Belinda whispered.

"Hear what?" Elda replied in a soft voice.

"There's a big storm to the east. The drifting snow has closed the tracks. Christopher and Joseph may not make it back tonight."

"Oh, no!" gasped Elda.

"They left the Brunswick station a while ago and headed west into the storm. That's all I know."

"This is terrible. The kids will be so disappointed. They really wanted Joseph to see them in the pageant. And their hearts will be broken if he's not home for Christmas. Did you hear anything else? Have they been heard from?

"That's all I heard, Elda. I'm as much in the dark as you."

"I'm really worried, Belinda."

"Shhhhh!" someone protested their whispers, undoubtedly unaware of the worrisome nature of the conversation.

Elda turned around. Her expression was blank as she tried to comprehend the details of the conversation with Belinda. Her heart raced. She looked at the crucifix that adorned the wall at the front of the church, and she prayed for her husband's safety.

The doors of the church opened with each late arrival, and each time, Joseph's children anxiously looked to see if it was their father. Time after time, throughout the pageant, they were disappointed.

"Where's Daddy," Anna thought to herself. "He said he would try to be here. Mommy said he would be here too." She was very disappointed, as were the other children.

It was difficult for Elda to sit through the pageant. Hearing the Christmas music and watching her children sing the season's praises made her feel sad. She feared something terrible was going to happen to Joseph. She couldn't imagine life without him. She was afraid and wanted him close to her. She wanted him to hold her and make her fears disappear.

❄ ❄ ❄

The locomotive sat on the snowy tracks, steam spouting from every orifice. It made noises like the labored breathing of a large animal that had been shot and was struggling to stay alive.

Joseph signaled the crew in the caboose to come forward to the engine. He and Christopher climbed down from the locomotive to survey the situation. The cold wind drove the snow almost blinding them. The rapidly falling snow piled up at their feet even as they stood and studied their predicament.

"It looks impossible!" judged Christopher.

Joseph remained silent as he examined the wheels of the locomotive. They were embedded deep into the snow; the front of the engine was almost buried.

The rest of the crew made their way up the tracks to where Christopher and Joseph stood.

"Perhaps we made a hasty decision," admitted Lee.

"Well, we made the decision, and now we have to live with it," Joseph snapped. "We can either sit here for the night, or we can make up our minds that we are going to get home. I'm not giving up," he replied with angry resolution. He grabbed the shovel from Lee's hand and plunged it into the snow that surrounded one of the wheels.

"Let's get to digging!" said John enthusiastically.

The tired crew began to shovel the snow away from the trapped locomotive in what seemed an impossible mission to free the train. The wind and snow were relentless, stubbornly undoing whatever progress was made.

"We have ta dig faster!" yelled Christopher, who was already physically spent from shoveling coal for the past several hours.

Somehow, they managed to clear the snow from around the wheels of the engine. Lee, John and Tom ran to the front of the train and started to remove the snow that covered part of the locomotive; Joseph and Christopher directed their efforts to clearing the tracks ahead.

They all shoveled persistently against the tide of the treacherous storm, and make modest progress. Ahead, lay a giant snowdrift, presenting them with a challenge far greater than their meager manpower was capable of conquering. Frustrated and drenched with sweat, Joseph dropped to his knees in final desperation. He angrily looked to the heavens from which the snow was falling, and prayed.

"Dear Lord in Heaven," he shouted hopelessly.

Christopher, seeing his friend in prayer, also knelt.

"I ask that you hear my prayer," he continued.

As Joseph prayed aloud, the other men stopped shoveling. Lee fell to his knees, pulling Tom with him. Even John, a rugged free spirit who hadn't prayed since he was a boy, was on his knees in reverence.

"I humbly ask that You give us the strength of a hundred men, the courage of Moses, and the wisdom of Jesus. I pray that You help us reach our homes on this eve of the most blessed day of the year, so that we may be with our loved ones to celebrate the birth of Your only Son. I pray to Thee, my Lord, with all my faith and all my heart. I ask that You hear my modest plea. Amen."

The men rose and began shoveling without pause until they made some headway against the storm. Joseph and Christopher boarded the locomotive while the crew remained on the ground. They eased the train backward for several hundred yards as the crew walked alongside. Joseph ordered John and Tom to uncouple the cars behind of the coal car.

Christopher began to stoke the fire again, heaving more coal into the mouth of the hungry locomotive to generate steam. The black nuggets immediately turned a glowing red as the intensity of the flames grew. The blaze roared from the firebox, instantly heating the cab. The locomotive snorted like an angry bull, panting heavily with unbridled determination.

"More coal, Christopher!" Joseph barked, knowing they would need all the power they could muster to break through the drift.

Joseph was about to employ a tactic known as "snowbucking": ramming the locomotive head-on into the snowdrift in an attempt to plow through it. He inched the throttle forward.

Slowly, the locomotive began rolling down the tracks, spewing white steam and gray smoke.

Joseph gave it more throttle and the engine lurched forward. Then he pushed the lever forward until it clanged against the metal housing, an indication that the throttle was fully open. With all his might, he pushed on it even more, hoping to squeeze out just a little bit more power.

The heavy metal wheels spun on the tracks, determined to keep pace with the enormous power produced by the stream-driven piston. As they sped down the tracks toward the obstruction, Christopher and Joseph looked at each other and braced for impact, grabbing whatever was available to hold on to. The engine struck the drift with immense force, exploding it into a white cloud that rose high into the air. When the engine stopped, Joseph threw it into reverse and backed down the tracks to prepare for another battering. Over and over again the engine burst into the snowdrift, chiseling it away. Relentlessly, Christopher nourished the fire with heavy loads of coal, ignoring the intense pain he felt in his lower back. Joseph continued to ram the locomotive into the drifted snow.

"We're losin' pressure, Joseph!" yelled Christopher over the roar of the fire.

Joseph now realized they had a new problem, a potentially fatal one. All the heat and extra steam had depleted the supply of the engine's life-blood; water. Without it they could not make steam, and without steam, there was no power.

"There's only enough steam ta make one more run, else we won't have enough water ta make it back ta Myersdale," Christopher surmised.

❋ ❋ ❋

The mood back in Myersdale was solemn. The children were worried about their father. Elda tried to hide her distress for the children's sake, but she too was extremely anxious. On the sofa table was a basket of roasted chestnuts, mostly uneaten. The usual merriment of Christmas Eve was subdued by the obvious emptiness of Joseph's chair. Anna sat by the window, waiting for her father to appear, but he didn't.

Sis, Jule, and Boopie sat quietly on the floor, while young Dick lay on the sofa, half asleep, his head in his mother's lap. Elda stroked his head, more to sooth her nerves than his. The tick-tock of the cuckoo clock seemed to grow louder with each swing of the pendulum, a constant reminder that it was getting later and later, and there was still no sign of Joseph.

Elda felt the reassuring grasp of a pair of strong hands on her shoulders. She looked up to discover that it was Earl.

"It'll be alright," he said. "Dad will be home tonight, I'm sure of it."

Elda grabbed onto Earl's hands and squeezed them. Until now, she hadn't acknowledged that her oldest son was becoming a man. Earl asked Sis and Jule to help him clear the dining room table. At the head of the table, among the remains of the solemn Christmas Eve meal the family had eaten in his absence, sat Joseph's place setting, undisturbed.

Anna turned from the window and began to cry. "Daddy's lost, I know he is."

Elda patted the cushion of the sofa in a gesture for Anna to come and sit next to her.

"Oh, Mommy, I just know something bad has happened."

"Your Daddy will be home tonight. I know he will." Elda

wrapped her arm around her young daughter and snuggled her head against Anna's. Anna's older sisters came over to comfort her, as well.

"Santa will be coming soon," Elda said in an attempt to brighten the bleak mood in the room. "Why don't we fix him and his elves a treat?"

"That's a great idea, Mom!" Boopie said jumping to his feet.

"Okay. That's what we'll do then," Elda said. "But after that, it's bedtime."

"Bedtime?" Boopie protested.

"But Mommy, can't we wait until Daddy gets home?" begged Anna.

"No. He's going to get home late tonight." But in truth, Elda was wondering if he would be home at all. "And if you're not in bed when Santa comes, he won't leave you any presents."

After helping the children prepare the snack for Santa, Elda shooed them all upstairs and tucked them into bed. When she passed Anna's room on the way down the steps, she heard her prayers.

"… And God, please protect my Daddy and make him safe. I love him and I want him home for Christmas. That would be the best Christmas present of all. Amen."

Elda went downstairs and tried to keep busy, hoping to make the time pass more quickly. She removed the basket of chestnuts from the living room table and looked out the window. The night had grown still. The air was silent. The street was empty. There was still no sign of Joseph. She lingered by the window.

"Would you like some tea, Mom?"

"No thank you, Earl. Why don't you go on up to bed too. It's late."

"I'll wait with you, if you like."

"No. There really is not anything you can do."

"I can help you set up the tree."

"That's okay. I don't feel like doing that right now anyway. But thanks."

Earl went upstairs, but was unable to fall asleep. Elda went out to the kitchen and continued to find chores to fill the time.

❋ ❋ ❋

They all crossed their fingers. Joseph thrust the throttle open, sending the locomotive down the rails. Christopher and Joseph exchanged a look of determination. With one hand gripping the throttle and the other holding the handrail, Joseph looked like a cowboy riding a bucking bronco. His eyes were tightly closed in anticipation of the pending collision with the wall of white ahead. Christopher pitched one last shovelful of coal into the flames.

The impact was incredible, throwing everything in the cab forward, including Joseph and Christopher. From outside, it must have looked like a great explosion of white. The crash hurled the remainder of the snow blockade into the night sky like a giant tidal wave.

They had done it! Their last-ditch effort freed them from the icy bondage that had stood between them and a Merry Christmas with their loved ones. Elated, Joseph looked down at the men as they simultaneously hoisted their shovels over their heads in joyous triumph.

"We did it, Christopher!" Joseph shouted. He turned to congratulate his friend and share this moment of triumph, but found Christopher slumped on the floor of the cab, screaming in pain. He rushed to his friend's side.

"My back, Joseph! My back!" Christopher's large frame had finally given way to the punishment. Hearing that something was wrong, Lee and John climbed aboard the engine.

"It's his back," said Joseph, still trembling from his bout with the snowdrift.

"I'll be alright," Christopher said defiantly, trying to minimize the situation with a forced smile.

"Well, you're through working for the night. I want you to ride in the caboose the rest of the way home, as our first-class passenger!" Joseph said, returning his smile. "John, I'll need you to work as fireman."

Lee called out the window, "Climb aboard, Tom. We'll go back and pick up the rest of the train and then we're headed home!"

Joseph eased the battle-weary locomotive backward until the coupler on the coal car bumped into the section of the train that had been left behind. John and Tom connected the cars, while Lee and Joseph helped Christopher into the caboose. It wasn't long before they were homeward bound again, this time with clear sailing ahead.

The storm had ended. The last of the clouds blew past a full moon that lit a star-studded sky. The lunar brightness reflected off the snow, lighting the way. A new night had been born from the hours of painful labor spent fighting the monstrous blizzard. The air was now calm, a stark contrast to the bad weather of just a short while ago.

Joseph looked ahead at the clear path before them. He smiled as he thanked God for responding to his request for clear passage. John sang an old railroad tune as he humped the coal into the blazing fire that propelled them home.

In the caboose, Christopher, though still in some pain, began his recovery. Lee and Tom looked out the window at the fleeting shadows darting by. As the train snaked its way through the Appalachian Mountains, its crew felt like victorious warriors who had beaten back a powerful enemy into surrender, and they had.

Chapter XIV

Joseph was now long ovedue. As the in-bound train limped toward Myersdale, Elda was becoming sick with worry. She sat at the kitchen table and nervously drank a cup of tea. Then she walked into the living room for a look out the window. Back to the kitchen she went, where she prayed and drank more tea. She repeated this routine deep into the night. Reluctantly, she came to the realization that, in all likelihood, Joseph would not be coming home that night.

Elda decided to bring the tree in from the porch and decorate if for the children, a job she normally enjoyed, but this night did without her usual enthusiasm. She opened the kitchen door and went outside onto the back porch. She dragged the huge fir tree across the porch to the back door. Struggling to get the giant Christmas tree through the opening of the doorway, she was startled by the presence of someone behind her. It was Joseph. He tapped her on the shoulder as casually as if he was cutting in on a dance. While she had been wrestling with the tree on the back porch, she had not heard him come in the front door.

"Oh, my!" Elda shouted as she dropped the tree. She turned and embraced him passionately. "Oh, Joseph," she said through her tears. "I'm so glad you made it back safely. I was worried sick."

Looking very tired, Joseph held Elda close and spoke softly into her ear.

"There was nothing that could have kept me away from home tonight. I love you, Elda."

"Oh, Joseph, I love you, too," she said as she kissed his face repeatedly.

Joseph looked down at his petite wife. Touching her face gently, he wiped away her tears.

"Don't cry, dear. It's okay now. I'm home."

Hearing the stir, Earl came downstairs but stopped short of making an entrance. Seeing his parents in each other's arms, he did not want to spoil their tender reunion. He quietly tiptoed back upstairs and went to sleep, relieved that his father was alright.

"Here, let me help you with that," Joseph said as he picked up the tree. He carried it into the living room and placed it in the corner by the window. Elda began to heat his supper and fix a cup of coffee to warm his chilled bones.

"I almost didn't make it here tonight. I'm very lucky that I did."

"I know. Belinda told me you left Brunswick during the storm."

"Yes. It was probably a pretty stupid thing we did, but we all wanted to get home. We were fortunate that it worked out for the best, but it was touch and go there for a while."

They sat at the kitchen table while Joseph ate. He told her of his perilous journey through the snow. When he finished, he took his plate to the sink and washed it. With his back to her he said, "What do you say I help you decorate that tree?"

Elda looked up with shock, "Are you serious?"

He turned and looked at her. "Do I look serious?"

Elda smiled. "Don't move a muscle, I'll get the decorations."

Joseph helped her carry the box of decorations into the living room. As they hung the ornaments Joseph said, "I was afraid this was going to happen."

"What?"

"First, I get talked into going to get the tree, now I'm standing here in the middle of the night decorating it."

He reached over and gave Elda a reassuring hug to let her know he was only kidding.

When Elda stretched on her tiptoes to hang a ball high up on the tree, Joseph slid behind her and wrapped his arms around her waist, embracing her from behind. Smelling the sweet scent of her hair, he kissed the nape of her neck tenderly. Then, he kissed her cheek. Pressing his cheek to hers he whispered, "I love you with all my soul. No one could ever replace you in my heart. Do you realize that?"

"Yes I do, Joseph."

He lifted the ornament from her hand and hung it in the exact spot she intended. Then he pulled a small angel from the ornament box. Standing on a stool, Joseph reached high into the tree and adorned its top with the angel. Still standing on the stool, he looked down at Elda and said, "Merry Christmas, my sweetheart."

Her face broke into a beaming smile. Pressing her hands together in approval, she looked up admiringly, first at the tree, then at Joseph and said, "Thank you so very much, Joseph."

After Elda placed the children's presents under the branches, she and Joseph sat in candlelight, admiring the tree. The aroma of balsam filled the room, adding another pleasant dimension to the moment.

"The kids will be so surprised to see you tomorrow morning. They went to bed thinking you were stranded in the snowstorm. Anna has been moping around all day. I think she misses her ring.

Joseph reached into his pocket. "I have something to show you," he said, pulling out the ring he got for Anna.

"Joseph!" Elda exclaimed with surprise. "Where did you get that beautiful ring?"

"Shhh!" gestured Joseph, drawing his finger to his lips. "You'll wake the kids," he whispered. "I got this in Brunswick for Anna. She should have it after what she did."

Joseph told Elda how he came upon the ring in the small, dingy shop in Brunswick. He told her about the distraught woman, her daughter, and the woman's gift of the ring to Anna. Joseph became emotional as he recounted the story and the way it related to his dreams and to Anna's.

"Oh, Joseph. She's going to love the ring. It's beautiful. Someday we'll have to tell her the story surrounding it."

"This ring is blessed, Elda, as we are blessed to have a child as generous and sensitive as Anna."

Joseph went quietly up the stairs, sneaked into Anna's room, and slipped the ring on her tiny finger, careful not to disturb her sleep. It was late when Joseph and Elda finally got into bed. They would get a short night's rest before the children would awaken on Christmas morning full of amazement.

Chapter XV

The children rose early on Christmas morning, motivated by their curiosity and excitement. Boopie led the pack down the stairs on a reconnaissance mission, just to make certain Santa had found the house okay.

"Wow, the tree is pretty!" gasped Jule.

"Shhhh! Quiet down or you'll get us in trouble!" Boopie warned.

"I wonder who the big package is for," whispered Sis.

"Let's go wake up Mommy and Daddy," young Dick spouted off impatiently, "so we can open our presents!"

"I hope Daddy made it home okay last night," Anna said.

"Let's go see," Boopie said as he raced up the stairs.

The gang followed him to their parents' bedroom door. Boopie stopped to open it a crack and to peek inside. He turned to his brothers and sisters and yelled, "He's here!"

The children spilled into the room and jumped on the bed where Joseph and Elda were stirring awake. They mobbed their father, all giving him hugs and kisses and telling him how glad they were to have him home.

"Santa's been here! Santa's been here!" Dick shrieked. "Can we go downstairs?"

"Oh, yes, the tree's beautiful," Anna slipped.

"Sounds like you've all been downstairs already," said Elda

with a grin.

"Well, we just went to the bottom of the stairs to see if Santa had come," admitted Jule. "But we didn't look at anything, honest, Mommy."

"Well Joseph, what do you think? Should we let the children go downstairs?" Elda kidded.

"Well," Joseph played along. "I guess so!"

Boopie led the charge, leaping down the staircase, hitting every third step.

"Wow!" he shouted as he reached the bottom.

He went straight to the presents, looking for a name tag that bored his name; young Dick was just a few steps behind. The girls were more captivated by the beauty of the tree.

"Oh, isn't it pretty," Jule exclaimed as she stopped at the bottom of the stairs.

"Yes, Santa did a great job this year," Anna said.

Joseph swung his legs over the edge of the bed; his feet landed in the slippers that he had strategically placed on the floor the night before.

"Earl?" he shouted, then waited for a response. As usual, there was none.

"Earl!" he shouted louder.

"What, Dad?" replied a sleepy voice from a room down the hall.

"It's cold in here. How about stoking up the fire?"

Still drowsy, Joseph and Elda made their way down the stairs to the living room. The room was filled with twitter as the children opened their gifts and played with their new toys. Joseph sat on the sofa with Elda and held her hand. They glanced at each other and exchanged smiles. The room warmed as Earl stoked the sleeping embers into a dancing fire.

"Look, Mommy!" Dick screamed, "Santa brought me a toy train, just like the one Daddy drives!"

Boopie was running around the house disposing of bad guys with the toy six-shooter that Santa had delivered. He brought his imaginary horse to a stop in front of Elda and tipped the brim of his new cowboy hat, "Howdy ma'am!"

Jule and Sis rummaged through the new clothes that Santa had wrapped in neat bundles and placed under the tree. Anna rocked her new baby doll to sleep.

In all of the excitement, Anna still hadn't noticed the ring that Joseph had placed on her finger while she slept. Joseph found this quite amusing, and he finally asked Anna, "Notice anything different on you?"

"No," she replied.

"Are you sure?" he said with a laugh.

After carefully examining herself, she again said, "No."

Suddenly, Anna became the focus of everyone's attention. As Joseph's laughter became more obvious, Sis saw the ring on Anna's finger and shouted, "You got a new ring!"

Anna looked at her hand and discovered the golden ring. Her face lit up as she admired the ring in wonderment.

"Oh Daddy! Mommy! Look! Look! Santa brought me a new ring! A new ring!"

She was so excited that she began to spin around in circles, holding the ring out for everyone to see. Her sisters shared in her exuberance, as they knew how much she loved the ring she had given away to help the needy family.

The excitement settled, and Joseph's thoughts drifted. He looked out the window and saw that the Christmas Eve storm had added another layer of white to the frozen ground. The snow glittered brightly as the sunlight reflected off the surface. The wind swirled and plowed the snow into drifts that leaned against the house.

Soon Joseph would have to leave the comfort of home and return to work. Christmas was not a holiday on the railroad. Because of his seniority, Joseph was able to switch shifts this Christmas, which at least allowed him to start to work later than usual.

The fragrance of flapjacks and gravy found its way from the kitchen to the chair where Joseph sat. The pleasant smell claimed his attention. Elda announced that the meal was ready, and the Beals assembled at the table for a hearty Christmas breakfast. Joseph led them in the blessing. As Anna put her hands together in prayer, she focused on the ring. She wondered how Santa knew what she really wanted.

By afternoon, a settled calm had replaced the noisy activity of the morning. The early dawn wore upon the children like a sedative. Joseph sat in the soft chair in the corner by the tree, with Anna perched quietly on his lap. Together, they enjoyed the beauty of the Christmas tree and the Nativity.

"I wish you could have seen the Christmas pageant last night, Daddy."

"I wish so, too, Anna. I bet you all stole the show."

"I was a good Mary and Sis's song was real pretty."

Oh, how Joseph wished he could have seen it. He gave Anna a squeeze.

"Daddy?"

"Yes?"

"Are you still mad with me for giving my ring to Martha?"

"No. I'm not angry at all, Anna. In fact, I'm very proud of you."

"I thought you were mad."

"Well, at first, I'm ashamed to admit, I was a little upset. But, after I thought about it, I realized I was wrong. I'm sorry, Anna."

"For what?"

"For the way I reacted. It was a wonderfully unselfish thing you did, helping that family. I should have told you so that night. I'm ashamed I didn't."

"Oh, that's okay, Daddy.

Joseph gave her another hug and told her how much he loved her.

"It's strange, Daddy, how everything works out. I gave my favorite ring to Martha. I loved that ring, but I felt so good when I gave it to her. I never thought I'd ever get another ring like that, but look, just look at this beautiful ring."

"It was a kind thing you did, Anna. You gave Martha and her family a Christmas gift they will remember the rest of their lives. In doing so, you also gave me a wonderful gift that I will treasure always."

"I gave you a gift?"

"Yes, you gave me the assurance that you understand the true meaning of Christmas and the importance of the gift that God gave to mankind. The Bible says: 'Give to others, and God will give to you.' Indeed, you received a full measure, a generous helping, poured into your hands. That is what happened, Anna. You gave unselfishly to help another, and you received a gift of even greater value: the good feeling that comes from giving."

The cuckoo clock in the dining room sounded twice. The wooden bird's song brought an end to the festive day, for now it was time for Joseph to don his coat and hat and walk to the train station to begin another day on the B&O Railroad. He gave departing hugs and kisses to his family and headed out the door.

As Joseph was leaving, he experienced a very unusual feeling. He did not know quite what it was, but he had never felt this way before, almost as though something was calling out to his soul.

As he walked up the street, he continued to be haunted by the feeling. He stopped and turned around, staring emptily at the house he had just left. Warm tears welled up in his eyes. He noticed a slight blurred figure standing behind the haze on the window. A small hand rose to wipe the frost from the frozen pane. The sunlight reflected brilliantly on the golden ring, exploding into a spectrum of spectacular light. Joseph saw that it was Anna looking out at him. They stared at each other for a few seconds, communicating their deep unspoken love as they gazed into each other's souls.

Joseph smiled, and with a wave of his hand, he turned and began his journey up the snow-covered street to the train station. Anna watched him until he disappeared. Then, she stared at his footprints in the snow, thinking how much she loved him. She hoped he knew just how much.

THE GOLDEN RING

Anna looked down at the golden ring on her hand as it glittered in the warm sunlight that poured through the window. Nervously, she twisted the ring on her finger. She could hear the faint sound of a locomotive's whistle and knew it was her father's train pulling away from the station. She peered back out the window and watched as the cruel December wind swept away her father's footprints, erasing the last remnants of his being.

❄ ❄ ❄

"That was the last time I ever saw my father," Grandma said sadly.

"What happened to him?" I asked.

"The railroad stole him from us on that cold and windy Christmas Day. While running a heavy load of coal down the mountain, his train jumped the tracks on a sharp curve and rolled down a steep embankment. Sadly, he was killed in that tragic accident."

Grandma looked up at me with a faint smile. Her blue eyes filled with moisture. A tear spilled out and rolled off her cheek, coming to rest on the golden ring.

"For years, I never fully understood the real significance of this ring," she said. "It wasn't until I was grown and heard the magnificent story I just told you that I received a true appreciation for the value of this precious gift my father gave me."

Feeling somewhat exhausted from our journey through time, we sat there in silence, clutching each other's hands, savoring the emotions we shared. The golden ring was a Christmas gift that Anna has treasured throughout the years; a parting gift left behind by a loving father. But, as Anna will tell you, it is not the ring itself that she truly cherishes, for it is merely a gift of metal and stone. The true significance in the gift of the golden ring lies in the powerful lesson it teaches about the goodness that comes from giving.

Epilogue

The passing years have taken much from my grandmother, Anna Snyder. Time has claimed her mother, Elda; her two sisters, Sis and Jule; and her brothers, Boopie and Earl. My grandfather, Howard John Snyder, died on February 25, 1985, leaving my grandmother a widow. On December 5, 1997, death took her firstborn child, Joseph, who was my father. Dick is still with us and resides in Ashtubula, Ohio, with his wife, Arlene. He is one of my favorite uncles.

Though Anna is in her declining years, her blue eyes still have a youthful sparkle. Her memory is sharp as a tack and her heart is as big as it ever was. Yes, the passing years have taken much from Anna, but they have given her more. She gave birth to three sons who blessed her with ten grandchildren and eleven great grandchildren, all of whom love her very much.

After my grandmother told me her story, I drove from her house to Myersdale with my wife and two daughters. The town remains much as I remember it from my visits to see my great grandma, Elda Beal, when I was a small boy. Sadly, the years have snatched away the two-story house at 525 North Street; today, the site is a vacant lot.

As I stood there quietly in the snow in the middle of the lot, I could almost hear the excitement of that Christmas morning some eighty years ago, when Anna received the gift of the golden ring. The memories of that Christmas and the lessons she learned have stayed with her. Now that she has shared her story, those lessons will always be with us, as well.

Time will inevitably take Anna from us. But when she departs, we can all take comfort in the knowledge that our lives were made much richer because of her.